adventures with

PLOOX

Book III: When Ploox Was King

the Brothers Armfinnigan

N. F. Armstrong
with
David "Mo" Armstrong

TO PAT:

They did it!.

MoA

First published by Dog Ear Publishing
4011 Vincennes Rd
Indianapolis, IN 46268
www.dogearpublishing.net

ISBN: 978-1-4575-4262-6

This book is printed on acid-free paper.

Printed in the United States of America

Also by The BROTHERS ARMFINNIGAN

2012 Golden Eagle Children's Choice Book Award Winner

Adventures With Ploox
Book I: Risks, Wrecks and Roughnecks

From the moment he learns his dad is missing in the jungles of Mexico, Nicky Neill Carpenter knows it is up to him to track him down. Nicky Neill realizes he cannot attempt such a dangerous mission alone; he will need a sidekick. There is only one kid who comes to mind: George Plucowski, aka Ploox. Scorned for thumb sucking, pant wetting, and a chronically leaking schnoz, Ploox is stunned when Nicky Neill asks him to be his unlikely partner.

Filled with a cast of unforgettable characters, *Adventures With Ploox, Book I* finds a pair of small-town boys surviving highway mayhem, hopping a freight train, and enduring the unforgettable horrors of the Armadillo Ranch Camp. Together they face each obstacle head-on as they make their way toward Mexico. As Book I of this exciting trilogy draws to a close, the boys find themselves engaged in an adventure unlike anything they have ever dreamed.

Adventures With Ploox
Book II: The Way South

Join Ploox and Nicky Neill in their continuing saga; an extraordinary adventure populated by uncommon characters and unexpected events. Ride alongside as they make their way south to the border of Mexico and beyond. Thrill with Ploox as he encounters love and recognition, the bite of the jungle, and a face-to-face brush with death. Marvel as they fly with the amazing Voladores, confront highway robbery Mexican-style, and climb into a world above the trees with a mysterious host— the last known person to see Dr. Carpenter alive.

Travel down every twist and turn in the boys' incredible pursuit as they learn ever more about themselves and their world. Prepare to be amazed by the wonder of it all.

To Dad
Our hero. We would have come looking for you, too.

Part 1

RETURN
of
JAGUAR COMET

CHAPTER 1

*N*icky Neill felt the blood drain from his face. For an instant, he experienced the sensation of some part of him slipping away from his body. Then he heard One-Zero's voice.

"If your father is with the Lacandon, he's alive. And if he's alive, he can be rescued." One-Zero's words echoed in Nicky Neill's ears. As they sunk in, the part of him that had pulled away came racing back to the present.

"This is it. This is what we've been searching for all this time. Dad's alive, One-Zero, I know it!"

One-Zero looked on quietly.

"What happens next? What do we do from here?"

One-Zero raised a knee and folded his hands around it. "I'd say you and Ploox have done pretty well on your own so far."

Nicky Neill stared into the shadow that covered One-Zero's face.

"Up to now, Ploox and I have survived. We got out of every jam we fell into...even that danged Armadillo Ranch Camp. I guess you could say we learned to never give up." Nicky Neill heaved a determined sigh. "Ploox and I pretty much believe we can do anything now. Does that make sense to you?"

One-Zero nodded. "I've been cursed with that train of thought myself."

"We're going to do what we've been doing all along, and that's to follow Dad's trail. Once we find him, we'll do whatever it takes to bring him home. But if you think you can help us get Dad out of wherever he is, I'm all for it. I know Ploox will back me on that. Of course, it's your choice."

One-Zero rose to his feet. "Amigo, if I could have a son of my own, I wouldn't mind if he was a lot like you." His hands came to rest on his hips. For a moment he stood still; then he strode across the balcony to the railing and peered into the darkness. "Here's an idea. You and Ploox, and Jorge if he's up for it, go into Lacandon territory an' make contact with 'em, learn what you can. Maybe your dad is with 'em, maybe not. If he's there, work out a scheme; then you get word back to me an' I'll size things up." He turned away from the railing to face Nicky Neill. "If I don't hear from you boys in three days, I'll assume you stumbled across the temple an' that you're prisoners yourselves. In that case, I'll come lookin' for you."

One-Zero stopped talking to clear his throat. "Another thing," he continued. "Come morning I'll have a map for you, one that should give you a fair idea of the terrain you're going to be operating in. It's mighty thick jungle where you're bound, an' you won't do your pappy any good if you get lost, right?"

"Yeah, right."

"Keep this in mind," One-Zero continued. "All you want to do for the time being is locate your pap. The Lacandon are not headhunters, you know? They're peaceful folks who appreciate their isolation, but you will be movin' into their ancestral home...it's their forest, not ours. Let's not make murderers of them because we put our interests in front of theirs. Savvy?"

"Yes, sir." Nicky Neill experienced a chill between his shoulder blades.

"Good. One more thing. When you fellas take off tomorrow mornin', leave your animals here. You'll do better on foot. Besides, I might find a use for them before this is over. That okay with you?"

"Sure," Nicky Neill answered. "Our butts feel like they're about to grow new blisters on top of the old ones!"

"Then it's settled." One-Zero stretched and allowed a drowsy yawn to escape into the still night air. "You best turn in, Nick, an' let your body catch up to your plans. You boys will need all the energy you can muster come tomorrow. Helen will show you to your bunk. Good night, pard."

"Good night, One-Zero. And thanks again for everything." Nicky Neill stood up and waited for Dr. Xama to pass around the swing and move ahead of him. Before he followed after her, he hesitated. When he turned around he found One-Zero's hand outstretched, waiting. He took it and grasped it with pride.

"Night," he repeated.

"Night," One-Zero echoed back.

CHAPTER 2

*D*r. Xama led Nicky Neill off the balcony to a dark corner on the far side of the tree house.

"Here." She paused. A rustle in her skirt produced a match. She struck it against a rough surface and brought the flame to a candle nestled in an odd holder. "An Indian flashlight," she said softly, extending the shimmering lamp in his direction. "Mind the mosquito net, it's highly flammable." Before she turned to go, she asked, "Is there anything you need?"

"Listen!" he whispered. "Do you hear that?"

In the opposite corner of the deck, Ploox sounded like a sawmill at full capacity.

"Oh, my!" she gasped. "That is more than snoring! I can make some earplugs, if you like?"

"No, ma'am, I won't need them. I've grown used to it by now. In fact, I'm not sure I could sleep without it."

"I understand," she said.

"Uh, there is one thing. I want to thank you, Helen, for the hospitality, and the surgery, and well, for pretty much everything..."

"It is my privilege," she answered. "I know you would do the same for me. Besides," her dark eyes sparkled in the candlelight, "we are a family. Our common name is Homo sapiens, and without that awareness we are diminished. And when we are diminished, there is no limit to our shared tragedy."

Nicky Neill was not certain what her words meant. He was lost in the symmetry of her face, and the tone of her voice.

"Who are you, Helen?" His voice caught in his throat. "I mean, who are you and One-Zero, really? I've never met anyone like the two of you."

Dr. Xama did not answer him right away. Rather, she studied him, closely.

"Elaborate," she said.

"Um, well," he stammered. "I guess, I mean..."

"Focus your thoughts, Nick." Her voice was kind, yet firm. "Words begin in your heart; then they are assembled in your mind. And then they are released by your mouth. It is a complex task at best."

After a moment, he took another stab at it. "I've been wondering what you and One-Zero are doing out here. I've got a feeling you have a purpose, but I can't quite...unlock it."

Another interval of silence followed.

"We are Observers," she whispered. "Here we are observing the rain forest."

"Observing? How do you observe a jungle?"

"These jungles, and others like them around the world, are disappearing. This phenomenon is of great interest to us."

"Disappearing?" Nicky Neill labored to keep his voice low. "But how can jungles ever disappear? There's so much. I mean...it's not possible."

"Everything is possible, you said so yourself. As for the rain forests, it is mankind that targets them for extinction."

"I don't understand, Dr. Xama. How can such a thing happen?"

"The quest for land," she replied. "The demands of agriculture, the need for timber, the pursuit of firewood. And more and more, the effects of pollution make their own dreadful contribution. These great forests are dying along with an entire universe of life around the planet."

"But, how bad can it be?" Nicky Neill focused on his breathing in order to stay calm because her words were ringing like a fire alarm in his ears. "Helen, who do you and One-Zero work for?"

"We work for all of mankind," she replied. "It is our privilege to represent an extension of the highest order of humanity..."

"Huh? I mean, I'm sorry, Helen. I didn't mean to cut you off...it's just, well, I've never heard this before."

"As I told you, we are Observers. It is our mission to gather and record scientific data as it relates to planetary well-being." Then she offered a surprising postscript to her explanation. "One-Zero has been at this much longer than I."

"One-Zero?" Nicky Neill was caught off guard again. His new friend did not strike him as a scientist, or even someone who would be interested in important things. "So, how long has he been doing this?"

"Almost two hundred years," she answered.

"What?" Nicky Neill moved closer to Dr. Xama. "Did you say two hundred years?"

"I did," she said. "You are tired, my son. You are ready for sleep. We can talk more in the morning if you like."

Nicky Neill experienced a sensation like a weight settling upon his shoulders, a feeling that caused his mind to drift one way and his body another.

"Helen? Can you read people's minds?"

"No," she smiled faintly, "only their faces."

Nicky Neill stumbled backward and encountered the mosquito net as it gave way to his body.

"Here," Helen lifted the net high into the air, "place your lantern on the tabletop." He did as she suggested and then he collapsed into a hammock.

"Aaah," he sighed. "I'm floating, aren't I, Helen? I'm floating above the rain forest..."

"Yes, Nick, you are floating. Floating on the world."

Nicky Neill was aware of Dr. Xama's voice tapering into the darkness as he rose up on one elbow and blew hard at the candle flickering near his head. The light wavered and disappeared. He returned his weary noggin to its resting place. Images of a world where everything floated flooded his mind. Before he lost consciousness he perceived a random tapping, a billion fingertips rapping on a non-existent windowpane floating effortlessly in the world like everything else.

A steady rain cloaked the jungle.

CHAPTER 3

*R*agged streaks of violet and amber bled through the darkness above the canopy, signaling the arrival of dawn. A raucous chorus of birdsong reverberated throughout the forest. Nicky Neill's eyes popped open. He rolled out of his hammock and tiptoed to the dangling balcony where he and his hosts had talked the previous evening. He eased into the same comfortable swing as before.

Waking up above a rain forest was an experience that almost defied description. The notion of time did not suggest itself like it ordinarily did. With that thought, Nicky Neill recalled Dr. Xama's words about One-Zero's age. She did say two hundred years, but how was that possible? The more he knew about these two people, the less he understood them.

A booming, deep-throated roar suddenly erupted in the foliage below him.

"Aggh!" Nicky Neill vaulted from his perch. The hairs on his neck quivered at attention. As he edged toward the balcony railing, the air exploded with another blast. This time the scream was closer.

"Alpha male!" a voice announced over his shoulder.

Nicky Neill sprang off the deck. "Yiii!" He spun around to find One-Zero standing a few feet away, munching a banana. "Dang! You scared me, man! I was..." Another deep wail cut his words short. "One-Zero, a jaguar is coming at us! Why are you just standing there? Get ready!"

"That does sound like a big cat, don't it?" One-Zero strode to the railing and cast the banana peel over the side. "But it ain't. It's a howler monkey. He's scolding somebody, or maybe making threats. Follow me." He led the way across the polished floor to the stairway and tiptoed to the level below.

Nicky Neill followed him to another balcony. "There," he pointed, "there's the culprit." Not more than twenty feet away, a dark brown bundle of fur was cradled at the top of a cluster of willowy branches. Nicky Neill looked closer and saw a somber face. The creature's black eyes peered back at him before turning away.

"Wow!" Nicky Neill exclaimed. "He had me going. You know, we've heard that call before, riding through the jungle. It always gave us a chill. I won't go all to pieces next time I hear it."

One-Zero turned and ascended the stairs. He returned to the conversation deck and settled into his favorite seat. Nicky Neill trailed after him. "So, you ready for the day?"

"Yes, sir. I'm ready, all right. Everything we've gone through on this trip has led us to this point."

"Hmm." One-Zero nodded. His gaze swung back to the forest below and the breaking dawn. Just as the sun crested the treetops, Ploox and Jorge spilled from their hammocks and stumbled onto the balcony to join their friends. It wasn't long before Helen called them all to breakfast.

Between bites, One-Zero reviewed the game plan. Ploox and Jorge remained silent, but their faces betrayed their apprehension. Still, neither one of them wavered, neither one complained.

Once the last banana and final sliver of mango had disappeared, One-Zero bent low to the floor to retrieve a tube-like bundle, which he unraveled and spread upon the tabletop.

"Your map!" he announced. The three boys crowded around him. "Here we are." He pointed to the center of the chart. "This symbol represents the tree house, and these arrows show the route you'll be taking into Lacandon territory. You'll be moving in a westerly direction, mostly. Now here," he slid his finger to the south, "is a tributary of the Usumacinta River. If you cross this stream, or the big river itself, you've gone too far south." He paused to massage his chin. "My hunch is that the sacred temple is more or less smack dab in the middle of their realm. The main village," his index finger pushed away from the stream where it separated from the main body of water, "is somewhere in this area. You poke around in there long enough and they'll find ya. Any questions?"

"Yeah," Ploox spoke up first. "How long a walk is it?"

"Hmm." One-Zero studied Ploox's face. "Three, maybe four hours, I reckon..."

"That might be a problem," Nicky Neill interjected. "I mean, Ploox may not be up to this. He had surgery just last night."

All eyes focused on Ploox.

"Hey! Ah'm good, really! Ta tell the truth, Ah don't feel nothin'...it's kinda spooky!" Ploox pushed away from the table and proceeded to hop in place on his bad leg. "See! Ah'm gooder 'n new!"

"One-Zero," Jorge flashed a broad grin at his companions, "you sure you don't wanna come weeth us?"

"Yep, I'm certain, Jorge. I've got a few chores to tend to here. One of 'em involves a canoe." One-Zero focused on the map again. "Take a look at this symbol." He gestured to a dark rendering along the bank of the tributary. "This is a big wall of rock, a chunk of mountain, ya can't miss it. It's the darndest thing, it just jumps right outta the earth. Anyway, just west of that rock there's a giant cortez tree that towers over the stream. I'm gonna hide a canoe somewhere near the base of that tree. In case a need might arise for a boat. Got that?"

"Yep, we got it," Ploox said.

"Good, good." One-Zero smiled. "That's the spirit! I got no doubt you boys're ready for this. In fact, I believe you men are the only fellas suited for this mission."

"Okay," Nicky Neill said, "let's get our gear together."

"Wait!" Ploox had a concerned expression on his face. "What's a cortez tree look like, anyway?"

"Ah, good question!" One-Zero nodded in confirmation. "A cortez has yellow leaves...hard to miss in all that green. Besides that, this particular tree is a giant."

Everyone rose to begin preparation for departure, but before they separated, Dr. Xama joined them.

"Boys, I have packed some food for you to carry: dried fruit and meat, plantain chips and the like. I also refilled your canteens with fresh water. Can you think of anything else you might wish to have?"

"I can't think of anything more," Nicky Neill said. "Thank you, Helen."

"Yeah, me neither," Ploox added. "Thanks fer ever'thang, Miss Helen!"

"*Gracias, señora*," Jorge said, bowing politely.

"So!" One-Zero clapped his hands. "Round up your gear, men. We're burnin' daylight here!"

"Oh, Ploox!" Dr. Xama called out. "Let me have your cape. Please. I must mend a tear before you go." Ploox slipped the cloak over his head and passed it to her.

Everyone but One-Zero dispersed to make ready for departure. He returned to his seat and raised his legs to the railing. Then he began to whistle. This time he created an odd melody that filled the entire tree house and had a calming effect on all of them.

Before long, the boys reassembled on the observation deck. Dr. Xama was waiting beside One-Zero. Draped over one arm was the freshly stitched cloak. "Come, Ploox," she beckoned. Ploox approached her and stood before her meekly, arms at his side. She draped the cape over his shoulders and adjusted the drawstring. "There!" She stepped back to admire the effect. "Ploox, you are royalty, quite clearly!"

"Don't forget this, Prince!" One-Zero swung an arm from behind his back, exposing the headpiece Margarita's grandmother had so lovingly made. He extended it to Dr. Xama, who positioned it upon Ploox's noggin. "Ah, yep, that's the ticket, man! All you need now is a litter and a squad of guys to carry ya!"

"One more thing, Ploox." Dr. Xama reached into a pocket and withdrew a leather thong. A curious stone was attached to the middle of the strand. She stepped forward again and stretched her arms around Ploox's neck. After knotting the ends of the thong, she backed away to stand beside One-Zero. "That's it!" she exclaimed. "The finishing touch!"

Nicky Neill and Jorge pressed closer to their regal companion to marvel at the stone dangling beneath his Adam's apple. Upon inspection, they observed a Mayan head carved into the stone. A serpent's body flowed from the figure's neck.

"It is a symbol of royalty," Dr. Xama explained. "Perhaps it will bring you luck. And, it complements the other stone you wear. I shall look forward to your return, Your Majesty."

"Oh, m'gosh!" Ploox moaned.

"What, Ploox?" Nicky Neill asked. "You don't like being a prince again?"

"Naw, it ain't that. Ah just had a thought o' goin' down that danged ladder!"

"Not necessarily." One-Zero grinned. "There is the fire escape! Grab your gear and follow me, gents."

The boys scooped up their bags and supplies and followed after their host. He led them down the staircase, across the first-floor deck, and toward the far side of the tree house. There they encountered a section of bamboo wall. One-Zero lifted a handle and slid the bamboo partition aside, exposing a catwalk that wrapped around the outer edge of the structure. The catwalk led to a short stairway that emptied onto an odd, circular balcony.

One corner of the platform was covered with foliage. One-Zero turned to face the boys. He was grinning more than usual. "You'll thank me for this later, men."

Ploox crept to the edge of the balcony and peered over. After a few seconds, he shrank back. "One-Zero, there ain't nothin' out there but air! I don't see no way down...no ladder, no rope, nothin'. An' I ain't jumpin', no sir!"

"I understand, Ploox, but you haven't seen this!" He waded into the thicket of vegetation at the corner of the balcony and pushed the branches aside, revealing a steel cable coated with a light green film. The boys watched as One-Zero used a rope to secure the branches away from the cable. "This," he gestured, "is the fire escape!"

"You've got to be kidding!" Nicky Neill murmured to himself.

"Whoa, whoa, whoa!" Ploox protested. "Whut is that darned thing, anyhow? An' whutever it is, Ah don't like it!"

"*Sí, señor,*" Jorge echoed, pushing himself against the back wall of the platform. "I don't theenk I like eet either!"

"It's a zip line," Nicky Neill responded, in little more than a whisper. "Am I right, One-Zero?"

"Right you are." His eyes twinkled in the gathering sunlight. "Until a fella's done this, he don't know what fun truly is!"

"*¡Aí, madre mía!*" Jorge's voice took on the accent of a whimper. "My freen', thees theeng no ees *divertido*, ees not fun...thees ees what I see een my nightmares, *comprende?* Weeth thees, chicos, thee eempossible she geeve way to thee loco. No, no, no...Jorge Campo cannot do thees!"

"Jorge." One-Zero stepped away from the cable and placed a hand on the boy's quivering shoulder. "From what I know about you, the impossible, the crazy, has never deterred your approach to life or business. Am I right?"

Jorge reluctantly concurred. "*Sí, tienes razón.*"

"Stay true to yourself, son. A thing like this, it shouldn't change who you are. *¿Comprende?*"

Jorge nodded and shuffled away from the wall. "So," he sighed, "go on, One-Zero. We all die sometime."

"Here's how it works, boys." One-Zero's enthusiasm increased as he reached out to grasp the cable. "This line of steel can support over 10,000 pounds, so don't be worried 'bout it giving way on ya. The ride down is fast, smooth, and simple. This here," he pushed his hand back to the end of the cable, "is what keeps ya rollin'." A cluster of metal objects rested upon the line. "You've probably seen these before? Pulleys, right?"

Three heads bobbed up and down in unison.

"Good," he continued. "This ring at the bottom of the pulley is what we hook on to." One-Zero poked a finger through the eye of the metal circle and tugged on it. "This piece could hold a water buffalo if necessary, but I ain't had the opportunity to test that theory yet! Anyway, here's the easy part." He reached higher up on the cable and withdrew a wide circle of rope. "This we run through the halo like so, an' then we double it through itself. Voilà! We have a sling! You just slip it over your head and under your arms and you are ready to fly!"

"Uh," Ploox interrupted One-Zero's demonstration, "whut happens at the bottom? Do yuh jus' plow into the dirt?"

"Hah! Ploox, that's the best part. The cable levels out and parallels the ground at the bottom. By the time you lose most of your momentum, you'll be able to touch the floor. Just run along 'til ya stop yourself an' you're there!"

"All right," Ploox sighed. "Who's gonna go first?"

"I reckon I'll be last," One-Zero said. "In case someone needs encouragement, ya know?"

Nicky Neill stepped forward. "I should go." He smiled. "My friends need to see that it works! Besides, I want to see Ploox's face coming down!"

"Well, there it is!" One-Zero threaded the loop of rope through the metal hole. "Like I said, you boys'll thank me for this later."

CHAPTER 4

Nicky Neill's companions looked on while One-Zero arranged the rigging. As the loop of rope tightened on the eye of the pulley, Nicky Neill slipped his head and shoulders through the circle of cable and raised his arms, fitting the line snugly into place below his armpits.

"Uh, Nicky Neill," Ploox fidgeted behind him, "why does the word 'noose' keep poppin' inta muh head while Ah'm watchin' ya?"

"¡Ai, hombre!" Jorge daubed at the beads of sweat that had appeared across his forehead. "Why you plant thees eemage een my head, too!"

"Oh, gosh! Sorry, Jorge, Ah wuz jus' thinkin' out loud." Ploox laughed nervously. "Ah'll keep muh thoughts ta muhself."

"There!" One-Zero tugged at the pulley. "She's snug, amigo. Ready for your rucksack?"

"Yes, sir." Nicky Neill lifted his arms and thrust them behind himself. One-Zero eased one shoulder strap at a time over the outstretched limbs until the pack was snugly adjusted to the boy's shoulders.

"There ya are, pard, ready to fly! Just step off the platform and let the harness carry your weight. Keep your grip on the rope right beneath the pulley and, above all, don't put your hands on the cable, unless you're hankerin' for broken fingers."

Nicky Neill cast a faux glance of bewilderment at his instructor.

"Okay, okay!" One-Zero laughed. "I had to throw that out there, don't ya know!"

Nicky Neill moved carefully to the edge of the platform and peered down into a green abyss. "Wow!" he mouthed. "¡Dios mio!" Jorge blurted. "¡Vaya con Dios!" He tried to turn away so as not to look, but he couldn't help himself. "Hey!" Ploox announced. A joyful expression was plastered across his face. "Dang, Nicky Neill, we're pole flyers! This ain't nothin' compared ta that ride!"

"Ploox, you're right! I didn't think about that. Here we are, voladores again, only this time no one's blackmailing us into thin air."

Nicky Neill edged his toes over the lip of the balcony and studied the cable's path. Try as he might, he could not discern the passageway. He did spy the horses and the donkey below. They appeared no larger than skinny dogs.

"Okay," he announced, "I'm going. I'll be waiting for you guys down below. Remember, if One-Zero says it's okay, then there's no reason for doubt." He looked his friends over. Ploox was pale, but beaming. Jorge was trembling and his eyes appeared glazed, but he nodded in agreement. "It's been nice knowing you, boys!" With that, he fell forward and disappeared.

CHAPTER 5

*N*icky Neill experienced a falling sensation as his weight wrested the cable's slack. His stomach plummeted to his feet, but immediately catapulted into his throat when the cable rebounded.

"Yeeeee-haaaaa-oooie! Whoop-a-coo!" He saw everything around him and below him. He even spotted the dark blob of a howler monkey resting in the canopy. Then his rocket descent gave way to an evening out and a course that paralleled the forest floor. He briefly skimmed over the low-lying vegetation before he found himself running, at first on empty air and then on the soft earth.

"Ho-leeee cow!" he shrieked as he came to a stop. "It's incredible! You guys are gonna love it! Ploox! Bring it down, man! Bring it down!"

Nicky Neill stared skyward, hoping to catch sight of Ploox, but the mass of vegetation was impenetrable. As minutes ticked by he began to worry that his friend had refused to step off the platform. Then the cable quivered and began to bob up and down.

"Kai-yaaaaaaa! Eeeeee-yow! Aghhhhh! Maaaaa-ma!" Seconds later, Ploox appeared overhead, descending at breakneck speed. From the ground he looked to be almost upside down, his legs thrust into the air, tighty-whities reflecting dappled sunshine, and his backside parallel to the jungle floor.

"Aaaaah-heeee-yip-eeeee! Yip! Yip! Yip!"

In a flash, his legs dropped beneath him and he commenced to run, churning the air in a foot race that only he envisioned. When his sandals did strike the earth, his acceleration only increased.

Twenty yards from where Nicky Neill stood grinning, Ploox came to rest, laughing and gasping like a madman.

"Ploox, you did it!" Nicky Neill rushed to his partner to help him get free of the harness.

"Oh, muh gosh, Nicky Neill! That was way more fun than pole flyin'! Ah think Ah could even..." Ploox's words were cut short by a woeful wail splintering the air above them. "Jorge!" Ploox pointed frantically. "Oh, muh gosh! Ah ain't sure he's even on the cable! Lookit, Nicky Neill."

Jorge did not appear to be gliding downward. Instead, his legs were flailing wildly and his arms flapped furiously at his sides.

"Dang!" Nicky Neill exclaimed. "He's trying to fly!"

"¡No más! ¡No más!" Jorge shrieked as he sped like a cannonball over their heads. "¡Páreme! ¡Páreme, por favor!"

By the time Ploox and Nicky Neill caught up to him, he was dangling a half-foot above the ground, laughing deliriously.

"Down, muchachos! Get me down!" Ploox took the cable with two hands and put his weight on it, bringing

"Together overcoming their fear, the boys zip through the air"

19

Jorge's feet to the forest floor. Nicky Neill quickly wrested his friend's bag from his shoulders and freed him from the harness. Jorge collapsed to the earth and began making snow angels in the carpet of leaves and ferns. "I tell you...I tell you, mis amigos...you hafta shoot me before I ever do thees theeng again! But I gotta tell ya," he bounced up from the jungle floor and clutched at his companions, "I reely wanna do thees again!"

The whine of the pulley racing over the cable suggested One-Zero's descent. A single "yee-haw!" confirmed their hunch. Seconds later he touched down the way a passenger plane strikes the runway—smoothly and under control. He slipped free of the rigging and turned toward the trio.

"Well?" he called out, walking back to where the boys had gathered. "Don't that beat going down a ladder?"

CHAPTER 6

"Let's keep our momentum goin', men," One-Zero announced. "I'll take the lead for a spell. Stay with me." He turned away and set off at a determined pace.

Nicky Neill fell in behind One-Zero, followed by Ploox. Jorge brought up the rear, still bubbling over with joy and adrenaline from their breathtaking descent.

Judging by the sun's position, Nicky Neill estimated they had been trekking for almost an hour when One-Zero pulled up. He waited until all three boys were gathered around him.

"Lads, this is where we part company."

"Yer goin' back already?" Ploox gasped between breaths. "We're jus' gettin' warmed up!"

"Got to," One-Zero replied. "I wanted to get you fellas off to a good start and I've done that. Now it's up to you guys to keep the pace. Don't allow any dawdlin'! Time may be a precious commodity at this point. Above all," he looked into each traveler's eyes, "no talkin'. Keep your ears and eyes open and your mouths shut. Got it? This ain't a good time to cross paths with any more tomb robbers."

"Yes, sir." Nicky Neill extended his hand. "We got it, One-Zero."

In succession, Ploox and Jorge shook hands with their friend. But Ploox had a final question.

"Hey, One-Zero! I gotta ask yuh somethin'."

"Sure, pard, ask away."

"Well...how come yuh got a name like One-Zero? Ah ain't never knowed anyone with a number fer a name before."

The permanent grin on One-Zero's face widened. "Ploox, ten is my lucky number, see? I was born on the tenth of October. I was the tenth kid in a family of ten. And the list goes on!

When I took the job I got now, I was given the chance to rename myself. Guess what day it was when that opportunity came knockin'?"

"Hah!" Ploox chuckled. "Musta been the tenth!"

"Exactly! But rather than havin' folks call me Ten, I stretched it out, ya know? One-Zero's got a better ring to it, huh?"

"Hmm." Ploox grinned back at him. "That makes sense, Ah guess. Still, Ah'd like to know yer real name."

One-Zero winked at him and pursed his lips.

"Lord, Ploox! It's been so long I can't remember! However, I'll give it some thought while you boys are gone. Maybe it'll come to me." He nodded in the direction they had been traveling. "Go on, now. Don't keep the Lacandon waitin'."

CHAPTER 7

" *O* kay, Neek! You take thee lead now, thee daylight she ees burning!"

"Right, Jorge. Let's get on with it." As Nicky Neill began to push ahead, he heard a voice over his shoulder. "Huh?" He spun about. One-Zero was gone.

"Good luck, Nicky Neill. *Vaya con Dios.*" Helen's voice called out to him, softly but clearly.

"Did you guys hear that? Did you hear Helen's voice?"

"Nope," Ploox wagged his head, "Ah didn't hear nothin'. How 'bout you, Jorge?"

"No, *aminuevo*, I don't heer notheeng. Maybe ees thee breeze? Or maybe ees thee voice of thee *selva*, you know, thee jongle? She ees alive. You understand thees now, I theenk."

"Yeah," Nicky Neill shrugged, "it was probably the breeze, all right." He turned back in search of the invisible path One-Zero had put them on. "Let's go."

Nicky Neill didn't understand it, but he was certain that Helen's voice had called out to him. He heard her, if not with his ear then with his mind.

The boys kept to their task as One-Zero had advised. They seldom spoke to one another, and they maintained a steady pace. Machetes were seldom called upon to clear the path. Still, the humidity was oppressive and each boy was on constant alert for critters. Jorge did not reduce their anxiety when he mentioned how on occasion fearless jaguars carried off *campesinos*. Above all else, the most pressing thought on each hiker's mind was their eminent encounter with the Lacandon. Although One-Zero had described them as a peaceful tribe of forest dwellers, Nicky Neill and Ploox imagined natives who dipped their arrows in frog poison, pierced their noses and

23

ears with the bones of their enemies, and shrank the heads of anyone who invaded their territory.

An hour after their only water break, Ploox made an announcement. "Hey! Ah gotta go pee!"

"Sure, Ploox," Jorge responded. "An' we could all use some more water. Maybe we rest a beet, hey, Neek?"

"Good idea. Let's hold up right here. You know, some of Helen's food would sure taste great right now."

"Yeah," Ploox crowed. "Food...water...rest, now them's words Ah understand!" With a resounding thunk, Ploox's bag hit the jungle floor. Seconds later, he disappeared into the bush.

Jorge grabbed a container of water from his gear while Nicky Neill opened one of the bundles of food Helen had prepared.

"Ai! Aminuevo, I deed not know how hongry I was unteel you open that *bolsa*! Say, how long you theenk we been walkin'?"

"Hmm, two, maybe three hours. What do you figure?"

"About thee same." He nodded. "But ees hard to tell traveling like thees...thee jongle, she don't measure time like we do."

"Hey, guys!" Ploox called out on his return. "You notice anything diff'rent 'round here?"

"Not really." Nicky Neill shrugged, offering his friend a slab of dried meat and a slice of mango. "What do you mean?"

"Well," he hesitated, "look around! The jungle don't look quite so wild here. Am Ah wrong?"

Ploox was right, the area did have more of a lived-in look.

"Neek," Jorge extended a hand, "may I see thee *mapa, por favor?*"

"Yeah, sure, Jorge. Here you go."

Jorge unfolded One-Zero's creation and began to scrutinize it. While he studied the map, Nicky Neill and Ploox scouted their immediate surroundings.

"Holy smokes!" Ploox screeched. "Nicky Neill, you gotta look at this."

"*¿Qué pasó?*" Jorge asked.

"This!" Ploox pointed at the earth. "Look at this!"

To everyone's amazement, Ploox had discovered what appeared to be a road. He wrestled a broken tree limb from the foliage and began to push loose brush away from the hard surface beneath their feet.

"These here ain't just chunks o' rock, see?"

"Ploox, you're right!" Nicky Neill helped his friend clear an opening on the pathway. "These are blocks of stone, all right. And they've been cut or shaped somehow...they're all rectangles, and every one of them is the same size!"

"Who made this?" Ploox demanded.

"Ees an old Mayan road," Jorge replied, admiring the way the stones fit together so snugly. "*Mi abuela*, she tell me of thees roads een thee *selva*. She say long ago such roads go up and down and all across Maya land."

"Watch this." Ploox walked to the far side of the roadway. Arriving at the edge, he spun about on his heels and began stepping off the distance to the opposite rim. "One, two, three, four, five, six, seven, eight! Eight giant steps! That's, uh...how many feet, Nicky Neill?"

"Oh, well, let me see." Nicky Neill cocked his head and set about making a rough calculation. "I'd say at least twenty feet, maybe more." He turned to Jorge. "What's your hunch?"

"*Sí, lo mismo.* But what I reelly want to know ees why thees *camino* ees een such good condition, no?"

The three travelers peered into each other's faces. It was Ploox who spoke first.

"Holy cow! Somebody's still usin' this here road!"

Nicky Neill forced down a hard swallow. His chest began to tighten. For an instant, he could hear the blood rushing through his ears.

"Guys," he whispered, "we're in Lacandon territory."

CHAPTER 8

"*T*his is what we came here for." Nicky Neill's voice was firm. "We follow this road. Let's go."

The boys scooped up their bags and formed a line with Nicky Neill in the lead. Jorge took the middle position and Ploox brought up the rear. The trio moved swiftly upon the stone surface.

"Hey! Pssst!" Ploox called out as quietly as possible. "Wait up!"

Nicky Neill and Jorge came to an abrupt halt.

"Yeah?" Nicky Neill whispered. "What is it?"

"I wuz thinkin'," Ploox's head swiveled from side to side as he came abreast of his companions, "whut if this here road leads straight ta that sacred temple o' theirs? Ah mean, meetin' up with these guys is one thing, but gettin' captured sneakin' up on their holy spot, well...then someone would hafta come rescue us!"

"He ees right, Neek." Jorge nodded in agreement. "Maybe thees jongle sidewalk, she ees not thee best place for us to be?"

"Yeah, I hear what you're saying. This feels too easy, doesn't it?" Nicky Neill scouted their position. "At least in the jungle we had some cover. Jorge, can I take a peek at that map?"

"*Sí, amigo. Aquí esta...aí, no!*" A panicked expression swept across Jorge's face. "Thee *mapa*...thee *mapa*! I don't haf eet. I leeve eet back there where we deescover thee road. Aí, amigos, I lose thee *mapa*!"

"It's okay, Jorge." Nicky Neill clasped his friend's shoulder. "Calm down. We know exactly where it is, huh? We just go back down the highway and pick it up. No problem."

"No, no, no! You two stay here and rest. I go back and find what I lost. Ees thee fair theeng to do." Jorge slid his bag from his shoulder. "I go, you guys stay."

"Nicky Neill," Ploox called out. "Ah don't like him goin' off alone. Whut if he gits snake bit, er...worse? Ah better go with him."

"You're right." Nicky Neill's backpack fell to the roadbed. "Only it'll be me going with him, not you. So far, that leg of yours has been holding up like a champ, but let's not push our luck. Park yourself right here, put your leg up, and keep an eye on our stuff. We'll be back in no time."

Before Ploox could protest, Nicky Neill and Jorge set off down the trail. In a matter of seconds they disappeared from view.

"Oh muh gosh," Ploox murmured to himself, "it got lonely here way too fast!" He gathered the bags around him and began to study the jungle that seemed to be closing in on him. Then he noticed a singular tree not far off the road. The tree's roots, gnarled and twisted, rose from the ground in angry pursuit of the tree trunk. "Dang! This here forest is givin' me the willies! An on top o' that, Ah gotta go again. Bad!"

Ploox stepped away from the mound of gear and equipment and made his way toward the edge of the ribbon of stone. For a moment, he paused and pondered his next step before he reluctantly tiptoed into the bush in the direction of the strange tree with the disfigured roots. When a guy's got to go, a guy's got to go.

CHAPTER 9

When Nicky Neill and Jorge returned with the map, they found their gear stacked neatly in the middle of the Mayan highway. Ploox was nowhere in sight.

"First thee *mapa*, now Ploox," Jorge sighed as he searched for clues to Ploox's whereabouts.

"The big guy's hard to lose." Nicky Neill chuckled. "My guess is he had to go again...he wouldn't wander off this rock island unless he had to."

"Sí, I agree. So, we wait, no?"

Nicky Neill was about to recommend that they move off the road until Ploox reappeared when a strange feeling came over him. The forest had gone quiet. All birdsong had ceased; no monkeys chattered.

"Jorge, is it just me or do you..."

WHOOSH! The air over their heads was split, ripped apart by an invisible, violent force.

WHOOSH! WHOOSH! Two more explosions of wind erupted above them.

"What the heck! Jorge, what's going on?" Nicky Neill instinctively crouched beside the pile of bags. "Get down, amigo!"

"¡Flechas!" Jorge screamed. "¡Flechas!"

"Huh? What is it, man?"

"Arrows, amigo! Someone ees shooting arrows...at us!"

At that moment, Nicky Neill saw what Jorge had already witnessed. WHOOSH! WHOOSH! WHOOSH! A hail of brightly colored missiles whizzed overhead, slashing the air as they passed. One of the arrows struck a small tree in the brush on the far side of the road. The sapling split in half and the arrow continued on, lodging itself in a sturdier tree in the near distance.

"Oh, my gosh! Those things are four feet long!"

"They're behind us, Neek!" Jorge shouted. "Come on, we gotta run...thees way!" Jorge sprang from cover and bolted toward the jungle beyond the road.

Nicky Neill launched himself in pursuit of his friend, attempting to keep his head down and his shoulders even lower. At the road's edge, Jorge plowed into the vegetation, picking up speed as he maintained his depressed profile. And he was zigzagging, too, making for a lousy target. Nicky Neill copied his friend's every move.

A bloodcurdling cry pierced the air, followed by a dozen more off to their right flank. Then another burst of whooping shattered the air ahead of them.

"Neek! They got us surrounded!"

"Hide!" Nicky Neill yelled. "Hide, Jorge!"

"¿Dónde?"

Nicky Neill froze in his tracks, looking about frantically for a hole to jump in. Then he heard the undergrowth crashing down around him. They were closing in.

"Jorge! Jorge!" But his friend did not respond.

CHAPTER 10

$\mathcal{N}$icky Neill braced himself for whatever was coming. His breathing tightened and he found himself panting. He had become prey. Then he blinked and they were there.

Even though he had read about the Lacandon in Ace Lucas's books, seen pictures of them, he was not prepared for the real thing. They appeared so gentle in a textbook, but now they were swarming all around him. And the effect was not benign.

There were at least two dozen of them encircling him. They were naked except for a single strip of loincloth. Their faces were streaked with ghastly swaths of white and yellow and black. Their dark hair hung below their waists. Each one of them held a sturdy bow, fully drawn, with long arrows notched and ready to fly. But it was their black and penetrating eyes that most frightened him. Nicky Neill glanced from face to face, looking for a hint of compassion, but found none.

One of the warriors stepped toward Nicky Neill and waved his weapon in a repetitive gesture. At the same time, he nodded over his left shoulder.

"What?" Nicky Neill struggled to understand the man's intent. "You want me to move that way, is that it?" He pointed in the direction the guy seemed to be indicating. The warrior nodded his head. "Okay." Nicky Neill began to shuffle in the direction he had been instructed to go.

The boy kept his hands raised as he moved. The circle of warriors moved with him, bows still drawn. Then he saw Jorge up ahead, surrounded by a second group of Lacandon. He appeared to be just as fearful. As Nicky Neill approached his friend, the warriors merged and formed a larger circle, herding the two intruders together. A pair of especially fierce-looking Indians stepped away from the others and advanced toward the prisoners. When they reached the boys, they stopped, angled their arrows directly at their prisoners' throats, and pulled back on their bowstrings another couple of inches.

"Aminuevo!" Jorge hissed out the side of his mouth. "I am so sorry. I always hear thees guys are peaceful."

"I'm sorry I got you into this, Jorge. Really sorry."

"Well," Jorge swallowed hard, "I theenk it weel be queek."

At that moment, everything changed.

An intense rustling occurred overhead. All eyes shifted up toward the sound of the commotion. Nicky Neill saw an odd tree over his shoulder with gnarled, deformed roots jutting out in all directions. The leaves on this tree were broad and shiny, blocking whatever was causing the disturbance higher up. The image of a jaguar formed in his mind's eye. From the expressions on the faces of the Lacandon, it appeared they might be having the same thought.

An ear-piercing scream ruptured the tension.

"Eeee-ai-eee-ya-eee-ya!" The scream was immediately followed by a flurry of breaking branches and flying leaves. At that instant a form appeared in the air and slammed to the earth in the center of the circle. It was Ploox! Without so much as a moment's hesitation, he squared his shoulders, raised one hand, palm facing outward, and spoke a single, forceful word in pig Latin. "Opstay!"

"Lacandon warriors are dumbfounded by a royal specter"

31

CHAPTER 11

*N*icky Neill's jaw dropped. Jorge was awestruck.

Every Lacandon warrior jumped back. Their ghastly faces and widespread eyes reflected shock and utter surprise. Nobody moved.

Seconds passed. Then, right out of the blue, every single Lacandon laid down his bow and all of his arrows and flopped to his knees and began wailing. As they lamented, they bowed their heads repetitively toward Ploox.

"Nicky Neill!" Ploox whispered without turning his head away from the warriors. "Whut's goin' on? Why're they doin' this?"

"I don't have a clue, but it might have something to do with how you just fell out of the sky."

"Also," Jorge added, "eet might be how he looks...maybe to thees guys Ploox ees not een costume."

"Whatever it is, keep doing what you're doing, Ploox. Jorge," Nicky Neill added, "let's try to move closer to Ploox."

Jorge and Nicky Neill began inching toward their friend. As they drew within arm's length of him, the two fiercest warriors jumped to their feet and snatched up their weapons, leveling their arrows at Nicky Neill and Jorge as before. But Ploox stepped toward them.

"Ontday!" he commanded. "Ontday ouchtay emthay!"

The warriors meekly lowered their weapons and returned to their knees.

Nicky Neill and Jorge eased into position behind Ploox.

"What now?" Nicky Neill wondered aloud.

"Ah think Ah got it figured out," Ploox said, speaking over his shoulder. "Yuh remember the story One-Zero told us 'bout these guys an' how they been waitin' ferever fer them Mayan bosses ta come back?"

"Yeah, I remember that story." Nicky Neill paused at the weight of Ploox's insight. "Oh, man, you don't think..."

"Uh-huh." Ploox was trembling. "That's what Ah figure; it's the only explanation."

"*Increíble!*" Jorge understood it as well. "Sí, Ploox, they theenk you are thee Maya king come back...*aí, Diós mío!* We are saved...maybe!"

"Ho-leee cow, Ploox!" Nicky Neill ceased to whisper. "You're king, man. You're a dadblasted king!"

"So, what now?" Jorge asked.

"We wait," Ploox replied. "They'll git ta their plan."

So they waited beneath the gnarled, deformed tree that had given life to their latest predicament.

The same Lacandon warrior who had guided Nicky Neill to Jorge rose to his feet. His comrades continued their chanting. He picked up his weapons, then moved in front of Ploox and bowed respectfully. Having acknowledged the king he backed away, and as he did he shouted out instructions to the others. Then he dashed off into the bush.

A thought occurred to Nicky Neill as he continued to assess their situation. One of them had to escape. Someone had to get word to One-Zero. It couldn't be him; he could not abandon Ploox. That left Jorge.

"Jorge!" His voice had an urgent ring to it.

"Sí, Neek. *¿Qué pasa?*"

"You have to escape, amigo. You've got to get word to One-Zero. Are you up to it?"

"We are theenkin' alike, my freen'. Eet has to be me. What I cannot eenveesion is how, exactly, I'm gonna sneek outta heer."

"You know what?" Nicky Neill patted his friend's shoulder. "I think you just get permission from the king. Ploox, give Jorge a send-off, why don't you!"

"You betcha!" Ploox turned to Jorge and placed both hands on his shoulders. "Jorge, you're free to escape. Nicky Neill an' me'll be with these guys when you an' One-Zero come back." Ploox stepped aside and waved his friend away. It was clear that Jorge had been dismissed. "Ogay, ogay! Ogay!"

Jorge nervously backed away from Ploox. For effect, he bowed all the way out of the circle, past the ring of warriors. When he set foot upon the Mayan highway, he scooped up his bag and cast a glance at the scene he had left behind. The Lacandon remained focused on their new king; his departure was of no consequence to them. Nicky Neill, however, was still watching after him, nodding his head in approval.

CHAPTER 12

*T*ime passed, yet stood still. Nothing changed beneath the ancient tree. The warriors who encircled them continued to defer to Ploox. Their bowing and their utterances had become mechanically repetitive and rhythmic. The effect seemed to induce a trance among the Lacandon.

"Ploox," Nicky Neill spoke softly into his friend's ear, "we got lucky, man. We've got to go with this as long as it lasts."

"Yeah, right." Ploox swiveled his head over his shoulder. "Ya reckon they know where your dad is?"

"They know, all right. We just have to get them to tell us."

"How we gonna do that?"

"Hah!" Nicky Neill patted his friend's shoulder. "The same way we do everything...figure it out as we go!"

"Right!" A smile lit up Ploox's face. "That's whut we do best."

Gradually, the shadows in the forest began to lengthen. The sense of relief the boys had enjoyed started to evaporate.

Ploox was about to express his concern when he heard something in the distance. "Listen, Nicky Neill! Did ya hear that?"

"Hear what? I don't...oh, yeah! Yeah! Music! I hear it!"

"Drums!" Ploox laughed.

"And flutes!" Nicky Neill added. "And whistles! Lots of whistles!"

"They're movin' pretty fast, Nicky Neill. Ah betcha they're comin' down that highway."

The music grew louder, as did the commotion that accompanied it. Something, someone—a lot of someones—was winding through the jungle. They were coming for Ploox. They were coming for the king.

CHAPTER 13

A dozen brightly painted warriors burst through the vegetation. The newcomers carried war clubs that dripped feathers and reflected light even in the gathering shadows. They immediately pierced the circle of wailers and formed a protective formation around Ploox and Nicky Neill. The warriors on the ground sprang to their feet and moved into a line behind the others.

A long train of Lacandon came into view on the road. It was obvious by the way these men carried themselves they were important members of the tribe.

"Hey, Ploox."

"Yeah," Ploox interrupted his friend, "Ah see it. Them guys're dressed a lot like me! Only, they're really old."

"Uh-huh," Nicky Neill murmured. "And they look like they're taking this pretty seriously."

The column of dignitaries left the road and proceeded toward the boys. As they drew nearer it became evident that their clothing was not merely similar to Ploox's; it was virtually identical. The only difference appeared to be the feathered headdresses they wore and the length of their capes that dragged along behind them.

At the end of the file, a company of musicians generated a storm of sound that pierced the air and jarred the senses.

The procession left the roadway and continued, in ceremonious fashion, to stride right up to Ploox. The leader, who appeared at least as old as dirt, raised one arm above his head, and the entire parade stopped on a dime. All music ceased. With no trace of emotion, the headman shuffled closer to Ploox. He stopped when it appeared his nose would collide with the boy's. Through squinted, ancient eyes he scrutinized the newcomer. When his gaze fell upon the pendants at Ploox's neck, an audible gasp escaped the old man. It was as if he had been sucker punched in his abdomen. An odd, dramatic cry burst from his lips.

"*Xai-tash-xai-eeeelah!*"

The old man, along with every other Lacandon present, fell to his knees and planted his forehead upon the forest floor.

Ploox looked to Nicky Neill. "Ah think we're gonna be okay after all."

CHAPTER 14

*T*he newly arrived Lacandon did not hug the earth for long. The old man returned to his feet after a respectful time on his knees. All the others followed suit. He promptly barked out a stream of commands. After a bit of shuffling, everyone, except for the dazzling warriors who had constructed a protective pocket around Ploox, formed themselves into a human corridor.

The leader cupped his hands to his mouth and issued a series of animal-like invocations. His cry was followed by a mild commotion in the brush. Then another cluster of rainbow warriors appeared carrying a strange contraption supported by long poles resting on the men's shoulders.

"Whut the heck is that, Nicky Neill?"

"Hmm." Nicky Neill watched as the warriors who toted the device double-timed to the far end of the corridor of elders and skidded to a halt. The old man who had set them in motion shouted out another command and waved the party to him. This time they moved ceremoniously, marching in unison toward Ploox. "Okay, I got it!" Nicky Neill smiled. "They're coming for you, boss. That thing is a litter. You won't be walking, wherever it is they're taking us."

"Litter!" Ploox's face wrinkled into a mask of utter revulsion. "The king don't ride in no giant box o' cat scat! Huh-uh, no sir-ee, Ah got muh pride!"

Nicky Neill slapped his friend on the shoulder. "That thing, amigo, is a carriage. And I'll bet you it's pretty slick on the inside. In fact," he elbowed the guest of honor, "I bet it's the cat's meow!"

Ploox looked on as the action unfolded. It did not take long for the litter bearers to reach the old man. When they

38

stood before him, he turned to face Ploox, bowed formally, and gestured with a gnarled finger at the carriage.

"Well, here goes, Nicky Neill." Ploox stepped out of the protective enclosure formed by the rainbow warriors and headed toward the litter. With each step he appeared to grow more confident. By the time he reached his transport, he had assumed a dignified posture. Ploox paused at the open doorway and turned toward the senior Lacandon. Their eyes met. Ploox nodded approvingly, then climbed into the carriage. When he was situated he looked back to Nicky Neill and extended an arm toward his friend, beckoning with his index finger.

"Omecay, Icknay! Ownay!" he said.

Nicky Neill gasped in surprise. He had become transfixed watching Ploox approach the buggy, so much so that he had forgotten his own status, which had quickly evolved into a condition of separateness. Separated from Ploox, that is.

"Whoa!" he exclaimed. He lurched frantically beyond the pocket of warriors toward the litter, which had already swung around in the opposite direction. As the carriage moved through the corridor of senior citizens, those who had been passed fell into line behind the conveyance. Nicky Neill was instructed, by the business end of a sinister war club, to keep to the rear of the procession. As they approached the old stone highway, the musicians marched into position behind Nicky Neill. They promptly broke into an earsplitting symphony of sound. Nicky Neill realized that however far they had to march, it was destined to be a very long trek.

CHAPTER 15

*T*he procession moved slowly down the ribbon of stone. The entire scene would have communicated an atmosphere of sober gravity had it not been for the musicians. Their odd assortment of instruments added a layer of gaiety to the event. Nicky Neill shrugged and sighed in relief at the happy outcome of their union with the forest Maya. They were alive. And Ploox was king.

As the parade continued its course along the ancient roadway, Nicky Neill began to notice Lacandon who were not part of the official procession. He observed children first, then women, peering from the edge of the forest along their path. They were giggling and smiling, and all of them pointed at Ploox's carriage.

Beyond an abrupt turn in the highway, a bustling village came into view. A colorful and animated throng of people crowded the path of the entourage. By the time Nicky Neill was able to see the big picture, the villagers were already mobbing Ploox's taxi.

Nicky Neill edged as close as he could get. He relaxed when he saw the protective barrier of warriors who still surrounded Ploox. They appeared as fierce as ever, determined to protect the king at all costs. Nicky Neill found himself laughing. Then Ploox caught sight of him and waved vigorously.

Nicky Neill maneuvered around the outer rim of the crowd until he spotted a tree that appeared easy to climb. He scaled it and eased himself onto an upper branch that offered both shade and a view.

Ploox found himself surrounded by a sea of faithful new subjects. They all yearned to be close to him. To his credit, he did not disappoint them. He waved and nodded. He blew

kisses. He touched hands. He had become an otherworldly figure, a king, and a messenger from the gods. George Plucowski
was born for this role.

CHAPTER 16

*N*ew ranks of elders appeared. Although they looked frail and ancient, these men quickly integrated the delirious mob into the official parade. Now the revelers outnumbered the sourpusses. Nicky Neill bailed from his tree and fell in behind the band.

The Lacandon and their newly arrived king proceeded to wind their way over the timeworn stone. At a bend in the route, the villagers were flushed out of the parade, herded to either side of the roadway. There, they stacked up into a crowd again. As Nicky Neill approached the curve, he observed a pair of thick stone pillars in the distance. He instinctively crowded closer to the musicians, merging with their ranks.

In short order, the tail of the procession passed between the great towers. Nicky Neill gawked at the strange faces and inscriptions carved into the stone. Staring at them made him feel insignificant and out of place. Then his peripheral vision caught sight of something enormous in the foreground. He turned away from the pillars and focused his gaze at the image ahead. His lungs emptied of oxygen, leaving him gasping for breath. A mere stone's throw away towered the object of their destination: the holy temple of the Lacandon.

CHAPTER 17

*T*here are some things in this world that speak for themselves. The mountain of stone that stood before Nicky Neill was one of those things.

The temple occupied the center of a space cleared of all trees. It shimmered in the tropical heat like an odd jewel. It rose up majestically toward the wisps of clouds overhead, signaling an unspoken intent to approach the Mayan gods themselves.

Nicky Neill studied the powerful structure as he bounced and jostled among the clamorous knot of musicians. What he discovered was a gigantic pyramid so steep its upper reaches appeared to waver against the turquoise sky. But unlike the pictures he had seen of Egyptian pyramids, this one did not come to a point. Instead, the top of this monument had been omitted, and in place of a peak he observed a broad, flat platform. Perched upon that landing was a radiant, multicolored temple.

The official procession fast approached the base of the massive shrine. Twenty-five yards out the parade came to a halt. All music ceased as the leaders and the warriors, and likewise the band, formed themselves into concentric semicircles facing the stairway that led to the open portion of the temple.

As far as the Lacandon were concerned, Nicky Neill was invisible. He removed himself from the main body of the formal group and sidestepped off to the far corner of the gathering where he gawked at the man-made mountain that towered above him.

The temple at the summit was impressive. This building was three-sided with the front of the shrine left open. What stood out most was the blazing effusion of color. Everything was painted a radiant pink with the exception of the outer frame; it shimmered a strain of blue that absorbed the sunlight and pulsated like a neon sign. The effect was dazzling. Adding to the splendor, long streamers of gaily decorated cloth hung from multiple rafters and out jutting flagpoles. An unusual object inside the temple captured Nicky Neill's attention. He cupped his hands to the sides of his head and squinted to make out the shape he had somehow overlooked.

Recessed upon the platform, centered at the very heart of the temple's sacred space, sat a substantive object. Peering harder, he detected a throne in the image of a two-headed jaguar. It was carved from a single slab of blue-green stone. A gasp of recognition escaped Nicky Neill's lips. Such a bench could only be fit for a king.

CHAPTER 18

A series of commands, barked out by one of the headmen, brought the official body of Lacandon to attention. Even the undisciplined crowd behind them fell silent. The warriors carrying Ploox's carriage approached the first row of steps at the pyramid's base and stopped. The armed squadron who maintained their fierce barrier around the king's litter accompanied them. They all froze in place while a somber new group flanked them and took up positions at the head of the column. These elders, from their sandals to their resplendent feathered capes to their elaborate headgear, were otherworldly. Another command pierced the air and the newcomers launched themselves up the pyramid steps.

They moved upward in two columns, each progressing in single file toward opposite corners at the top. When all the men had reached the summit, they formed themselves into a circle around the jaguar throne and peered down at the throng below.

On cue, the litter bearers and their phalanx of warriors began their own ascent to the temple. Nicky Neill thought he witnessed an expression of horror on Ploox's face as his taxi began to bob precariously, but it soon disappeared. As he looked on, the magnitude of the sight he was witnessing struck home. How those men managed to carry a box containing Ploox straight up into the air without spilling him over the side was nothing short of spectacular.

In a brief span of time, the litter bearers and the armed warriors reached the platform. With great care, the porters lowered their charge to the floor. As the carriage touched down, several of the shimmering elders stepped forward, beckoning for Ploox to join them.

Ploox tentatively exited his transport and approached the men. Two of them held out their hands and he accepted their gesture. With the new king in tow, they proceeded toward the two-headed jaguar bench. When they stood before it, Ploox's guides gently turned him around and stepped away from him. Another elder appeared from the shadows laden with bundles of varying sizes. As he reached the boy's side, he motioned to the men who had delivered him. Together, the trio began sorting out the bundles.

Nicky Neill watched as the ceremony unfolded and it dawned on him that he had seen paintings of this very thing in one of Ace's books. The paintings showed a transfer of authority from one ruler to the next, only on this occasion the title of king was being conferred to Ploox, a title that had remained unfilled for the last five hundred years.

The bundles turned out to be protective covering that sheltered important artifacts. With considerable effort, the individual in charge stepped toward Ploox and rose up on his tiptoes. The boy stooped low to accommodate the man's intention.

The first stage of the ceremony involved the draping of a necklace over Ploox's head. Once he had accomplished that, the elder backed away and waited for his assistants to unwrap the next bundle. They worked slowly, signaling great regard for the object they sought to uncover. At last, the protective veil fell away and a multihued glow filled the opening in the temple. A uniform gasp rose up from the crowd of onlookers. Their exclamation transformed into a cacophony of wailing, howling, and outright weeping when the glow burst into wild explosions of blinding light. The elder struggled to gain control of the unwieldy thing in his hands, but it was more than he could manage. He called out for his helpers to assist him. Together, they hoisted a gargantuan headpiece above them and shuffled toward Ploox. Another elder appeared and delicately removed Margarita's crown. Then the three primary elders positioned the new headdress on Ploox's noggin. It was difficult for Nicky Neill to look at his friend as the new crown dazzled in the sunlight. It also partially obscured his face. The final touch consisted of a long green cape of feathers studded with jewels and mirrors. It was the perfect mate to the headdress as it sparkled and shimmered in its own right. The two assistants waited for their leader to remove Ploox's traveling cape, then closed in and draped the new one over the king's shoulders. When the cape was fastened at his throat, the elders guided Ploox backward to the jaguar throne. With all the grace he could muster, Ploox eased himself onto the bench and smiled broadly.

The three elders before him bowed low and then rejoined the others in the circle. From there, the entire group bowed in unison before dropping to their knees. The warriors on the perimeter of the circle then set about bowing before they, too, fell to their knees. From there, they plastered their foreheads to the stone floor and remained motionless. The mass genuflection spread to the spectators at the base of the pyramid. In

"Enthroned and shining: King Ploox"

a matter of seconds, Nicky Neill found himself the only person still on his feet. He, too, bowed and dropped to his knees. At that moment, he realized that it was official: PLOOX WAS KING!

CHAPTER 19

*N*icky Neill was hard pressed to specify how long the Lacandon remained on their knees in submission to the new king. His best hunch was five minutes. When the reverence ended one thing was clear—the sober, solemn quality of the whole affair had come to an end.

The villagers beyond the stone pillars began to chant. Their voices grew into a joyous uproar that escalated into a frenzy. Spontaneous dancing erupted. Parents tossed their kids into the air. And the musicians went back to doing what they did best.

While the festivities got underway, Ploox was escorted back to his carriage and lowered down the steep sides of the pyramid to the earth. From there, the official procession made its way beyond the pyramid and onto the stone roadway once more. Nicky Neill tagged along at the rear.

The organized procession transformed itself into a clamorous parade as the party fell in line behind the royal entourage. Nicky Neill scrambled off the road and joined a pocket of revelers. From there he was able to observe Ploox, grinning and waving like mad at his newfound subjects. It was hard to tell who was enjoying the moment more, Ploox or the Lacandon.

The procession spilled into a broad alley that cut through a tunnel of rain forest and channeled into a large, man-made clearing. As he entered the open space, Nicky Neill could see they were approaching the Lacandon village.

Row upon row of small, identical huts stretched as far as he could see. There were no doors on any of the structures. People and livestock wandered in and out. The furnishings were sparse, and every hut included an outdoor cooking facility.

The parade marched through the village until Ploox's court and bodyguards reached the far end. There the stately event ground to a halt. Ploox was immediately swarmed by a mass of enthusiastic admirers.

Nicky Neill attempted to push through the crowd to get closer to his friend, but an impenetrable human wall had formed around the king. In a panic, he scaled a pole leaning against a nearby hut and edged onto the roof. From there he could at least observe some of the action. No sooner had he settled in than a great cry arose from the mob.

In the near distance behind the king, a towering wall of vegetation fell forward. When it struck the earth, a tsunami of dust and leaves erupted into the air. Then a second wall collapsed, followed by another explosion of soil and debris. A hazy curtain hung in the air for a full minute or more. When the dingy cloud settled, another collective gasp escaped from the villagers. Nicky Neill found himself panting for breath. The awe that rippled through his body nearly sent him sliding off the roof.

CHAPTER 20

*A*n enormous silhouette took shape in the background. The image quivered in the dust-laden air until an avalanche of sunlight burst through the murky veil and revealed a building the likes of which Nicky Neill had never encountered.

"Hol-eee..." Nicky Neill gasped. Right behind Ploox, rising up a good three stories, stood a bamboo castle. Unlike the sea of huts all around them, this house was fit for a king.

The walls of the place were solid; no daylight spilled through gaping cracks. Real doors, with handles and hinges, signaled a departure from the wide- open dwellings of the common villagers. There were windows as well, and balconies on the upper floors. An enormous banner hung from the middle story. A bold, wildly colorful image spread across its surface. The scene on the canvas reflected the ceremony that had just occurred on the pyramid. The main subject in the painting looked exactly like Ploox. Before Nicky Neill could imagine what the interior of the palace looked like, an abrupt hush fell over the crowd. Ploox and his carriage were being conveyed up the steps of the main porch.

Ploox descended from his ride and was joined by three of the elders. Nicky Neill craned his neck to see what would happen next. His gaze was met by one of the officials beside Ploox. The old man summoned a nearby warrior. An exchange took place. The soldier bolted off the porch and sprinted into the crowd while the party on the stoop disappeared into the building.

The mob parted, creating a path for the warrior. In a matter of seconds, he was standing in front of the hut Nicky Neill had scaled. With no hint of patience, the envoy raised his spear and made a motion indicating that Nicky Neill should follow him.

The boy did not hesitate. He jumped from the roof and landed an arm's length from the elite bodyguard. Without a word, the warrior spun about and retraced his steps.

When they reached the palace stairs, his guide nodded approvingly. He did not, however, encourage his follower to step onto the veranda. Nicky Neill waited until the tall door creaked open. One of the elders emerged and beckoned to Nicky Neill. With the warrior's acknowledgment, the boy jumped onto the porch and slipped through the opening.

As the door closed behind him, the old man turned and made the "sssh" sign with a gnarled finger pressed to his lips. For an instant, Nicky Neill's jaw dropped. The elder was bedazzling. He stood cloaked in iridescent feathers from head to toe. Gold earrings, shaped like serpents, hung low from his earlobes, while a broad, polished jade choker ringed his neck and jade bracelets obscured his wrists. An involuntary gasp escaped Nicky Neill when he noticed the solid gold bone protruding from the man's nostrils. The image of the individual who stood before him would remain seared in his memory forever.

CHAPTER 21

*T*he shimmering figure glanced over his shoulder before he skirted a wooden partition and disappeared. Nicky Neill was left alone. While he waited he studied the anteroom he had been left to.

Overhead, an array of strange objects dangled from the high ceiling. As he studied the arrangement, Nicky Neill realized he was observing an astronomical map. What next captured his attention was the pungent fragrance of incense that saturated the closed space. Before he could look any further, the multicolored elder reappeared from behind the partition and signaled the visitor to follow after him.

Nicky Neill made his way around the ornate barrier, close on the heels of his guide. Another room, larger than the entryway, confronted him. In the middle of the broad, open space, a cluster of elders sat cross-legged on the polished floor, eyes closed. With an obvious display of reverence, Nicky Neill's guide escorted him around the others and into a narrow hallway at the back of the room. At the hallway's end the old man parted a curtain of living flowers, exposing a wide stairwell. Nicky Neill's escort paused and glared at his charge. Then, with amazing agility, he turned and launched his ascent.

They climbed twenty-seven well-polished steps that delivered them to another narrow hallway. The passageway exploded with color. Bold murals covered the walls depicting people and animals in larger-than-life dimensions.

As he passed through the riotous corridor, Nicky Neill encountered another great room. The walls of this chamber portrayed a 360-degree odyssey of historical drama punctuated with beauty and violence and oddly grotesque manifestations of otherworldly beings and events.

The power of the murals was overwhelming. Nicky Neill's mind was forced to compact centuries of Mayan history into mere seconds. Just as he was about to crumple to the floor, his guide clasped him by the shoulder and barked a single command, pointing with an arthritic finger to the last panel at the far corner of the room. The paint on this section of the wall was so fresh it glistened in the light of day. An unintended snort of laughter escaped his lips. The final panel of painted history depicted the coronation of a new ruler. On closer inspection, it was clear beyond doubt who that ruler was.

For once, Nicky Neill's guide smiled, revealing a set of teeth that no dentist on earth would touch. The old man continued to gesture at the coronation scene. At this point, he was uttering a stream of words in a language so foreign they could have been extraterrestrial.

As soon as the elder started talking, another noise erupted across the room. The outburst, a harsh cackling sound, was accompanied by a frenzied flapping of wings as a pair of quetzals detached themselves from a portion of the mural and flew to a rafter overhead.

Ace had spoken of the quetzal and the significance the bird had to the Maya. The two creatures above him were the most beautiful animals Nicky Neill had ever seen. Their tails consisted of two or more feet of shimmering feathers that trailed away from a body engulfed in magnificent, iridescent color. Staring at them felt almost rude. When he looked away he caught sight of his guide observing the birds. The old man puffed his chest and shook his entire body. In that moment Nicky Neill understood more about the Maya than he could ever learn from a book.

The pair of birds swooped down from their ceiling perch and landed in perfect unison on an invisible roost that extended from a panel of the mural. They blended into the painting so effortlessly that it appeared the scene had swallowed them up. They were magical creatures indeed, symbols of royalty like nothing else could be. Then someone called out to him.

CHAPTER 22

" *N* icky Neill!"

"Huh?" Nicky Neill jumped back, certain the nearest panel of mural was speaking to him.

"Over here, behind the curtain!"

At the far end of the room, another illusion materialized. What had been perceived as a blank wall turned out to be a densely woven curtain of fine cloth. Nicky Neill squinted hard at the veil that began to ripple as a breeze passed through the empty space. He approached the curtain in tentative fashion, expecting his guide to check his progress any second. At the curtain's edge, Nicky Neill extended an arm and swept the cover back. There sat Ploox, his face appearing and reappearing behind a pair of enormous green leaves. Two young girls clutched the leaves' stalks, waving them with obvious devotion in alternating motions.

"Come on in, Nicky Neill!" Ploox's voice strained to conceal his urge to laugh.

"What the—" For an instant, Nicky Neill was taken aback. It was Ploox all right, but not the guy he had spent the last three weeks with. His old buddy was decked out like the grand pooh-bahs who ran the show for the Lacandon. Only Ploox's wardrobe was more resplendent than the rest. The transformation was complete; Ploox was a bona fide, dyed-in-the-wool king!

"Hey, quit starin', it's me!" Ploox finally burst out in laughter. "Come on over here, we gotta talk."

Nicky Neill stepped away from the curtain and positioned himself in front of His Highness in order to make eye contact. That proved to be difficult as the girls were bent on doing their job. "Uh, this fan stuff is makin' me dizzy. Can yuh get them ta back off?"

"Opstay! Opstay!" Ploox commanded, waving the fans away. Blushing and giggling, the girls laid their fans at the king's feet and scampered out of the room.

"Whew! That's better. Them leaves're gonna give me a headache, er worse."

"Do they always do that?" Nicky Neill wondered.

"Well, they ain't stopped since Ah plopped down in this here chair."

"Hah! What's it like being a king?"

"Busy!" Ploox blurted between chuckles. "Ever since they snatched me up in that shoulder boat, it's been all go, go, go! Heck, you've seen it! Ah been hustled down the road, up the pyramid, down the pyramid, up the road again, through the village, and into this here castle ... an' jus' when Ah think Ah might have a sec ta scratch muh nose, in comes a pair o' them ol' peacocks blabberin' their lingo an' wavin' their arms. At some point," he glanced around furtively, "Ah'm gonna hafta pee! Whut then? An' by the way, Ah'm mighty glad ta see ya."

"Yeah, me too. I get real nervous when they whisk you away."

"Whut's next?" Ploox's tone became more serious. "Ah reckon Ah kin pull off playin' king fer a spell, but in the long run it's bound ta git tricky, ya know?"

"That's a great question. Right now I'm not sure what our next step will be." Nicky Neill paused and glanced over his shoulder. While his guide was partially obscured by the curtain, he was monitoring their exchange with serious intent. "I'm afraid we'll have to play it by ear for a day or so, you know, to give me some time to check things out. I've got a feeling in my gut that my dad was here."

Ploox nodded in agreement. As his head wagged, the glorious feathers in his headdress rippled and shimmered across his forehead.

"I've got to discover some sign of Dad being here," Nicky Neill continued. "Right now I'm thinking that if I can find any of those prisoners they say the Lacandon keep, I could uncover some clues. I mean, all these people got a good look at me today, right? I'm sure someone put eyeballs on my dad."

Ploox's familiar grin spread across his face. "Lookit, Nicky Neill, Ah kin pull off this king thing fer a spell. Purty much ever'thang Ah do is okay 'cause these here folks is so darned happy ta have me. But Ah do see a few dark clouds on the horizon." Ploox's expression grew serious, and for an instant he appeared older, wiser. "Sometime soon," he went on, "them old guys is gonna expect some stuff from me, ya know, magic, miracles, and such. Once they figure out Ah ain't heaven sent, they ain't gonna like me so much. Know whut Ah mean?"

"Yeah, yeah, I do."

"Hey, Nicky Neill, yuh reckon Jorge's okay?"

"Oh," he responded without a hitch, "I know he got away. I'm sure of it, aren't you?"

"Yeah," Ploox sighed. "He's too smart ta git nabbed a second time."

At that moment, Lacandon voices rang out from the stairwell. The echo of footsteps signaled the party's imminent arrival.

"Keep doing what you're doing, pal. It seems to be working just fine."

CHAPTER 23

"*H*ere they come," Ploox whispered. "You take care of yerself. Don't worry 'bout me none. Ah'll be right here more'n likely."

A group of stone-faced elders filed into the chamber behind the curtain as Nicky Neill stepped away from the king. Out of the corner of his eye, he observed Ploox straightening up in his chair, assuming a more regal posture.

"Pssst!" A sharp hissing noise issued from the far side of the curtain. Nicky Neill's somber guide beckoned that he move away from the throne. He obeyed. As he cleared the curtain, the two fan girls reappeared, leaves in hand, pushing him aside in their haste to return to their duties.

Nicky Neill followed Quetzal Man onto a wide porch at the rear of the palace. Without a word, the old man showed him outside and bolted the door behind him.

Outside, the air was heavy with smoke and humidity. At that moment Nicky Neill realized how thirsty and hungry he was. He skirted the corner of the palace and headed toward the village. As he ambled along the central pathway, he heard the sounds of music and singing in the distance. Where there was festivity, there would be food.

At the center of the deserted village, he lingered in the open common space. Then the notion struck him. He sensed he was being followed. He imagined Quetzal Man was tailing him. Out of orneriness more than anything else, he scurried across the opening and ducked into an empty hut.

Seconds passed and a figure emerged on the far side of the clearing. It was not Quetzal Man. The Lacandon made his way across the open space, and Nicky Neill observed he was not wearing the typical loincloth that most men seemed to prefer.

This person was cloaked in a long white tunic. Perhaps it was a woman? As casually as possible, Nicky Neill stepped from his hut and addressed the stranger.

"Hey there, you looking for me?"

The individual did not so much as flinch. Instead, he turned toward Nicky Neill and responded in perfect English.

"Oh, there you are."

"Huh? You speak English?"

"Yes, of course," he answered. "I also speak Spanish and French, and I read Latin. But I don't use them much anymore."

When the man reached Nicky Neill, he stopped and offered his hand. "Please forgive me for following you. I hope I didn't frighten you?"

"No, no, sir. Don't worry about it."

"My name is Hector Villaverde de Leon, formerly chief petroleum engineer of Montebello Petroleum Company, presently ordinary Lacandon citizen." He bowed slightly at the end of his introduction.

"Pleased to meet you, Hector. My name is Nicky Neill Carpenter. I'm here to..."

"Look for your father, correct?" Hector smiled faintly. "The resemblance is clear."

Nicky Neill was flabbergasted...and speechless.

"Don't be alarmed." Hector placed a hand on Nicky Neill's shoulder. "I've been expecting someone for weeks now, but I anticipated an army unit or an American delegation. I must say, I never considered the outside world would send a pair of boys to rescue a man of your father's stature."

"You KNOW my father?"

Hector hesitated, gathering his thoughts. "I did not actually meet your father, not formally. We never spoke as you and I are now...he was too closely guarded. Besides, he wasn't in the village more than a couple of days."

"Why not?" Nicky Neill's excitement dissolved into frustration. "What did they do to him? Where did he go? What happened?"

"Please, son, don't be upset. I'm not sure where your father is now, but while he was here they treated him well. Mysterious events are..."

"Hector!" Nicky Neill was gasping for air. "Hector, we've got to have a serious talk! I need to learn everything you know about my dad. There's no time to waste!"

"Yes, of course, I agree." A hint of distress crept into Hector's tone. "But this is not the place. Come to my hut; we can talk freely there. I will share with you all that I know. Come!"

Hector led the way with Nicky Neill trailing close behind. They walked through the village, beyond the main body of huts and activity clearings, to the outskirts of the settlement.

"There," Hector pointed, "that is my home." Nicky Neill peered around him and spotted the shadowy outline of a structure silhouetted against the jungle. It stood alone, apart from a few others at the end of the footpath.

"It's different, isn't it?" Nicky Neill said, squinting into the distance for a better look.

"It is different, my friend." Hector chuckled. "There is no other Lacandon house quite like it. Notice I have built two stories."

"Yeah, I see that. I also see doors and windows and walls that appear to be solid. Your place looks like a real house!" By that time the two were standing at the front door.

When Nicky Neill set foot inside the house, a wooden floor creaked beneath his weight. An oil lamp hung from a rafter in the middle of the room, burning brightly. On closer inspection, Nicky Neill noted a rug and well-made furniture as well as several freestanding lamps.

"How did you end up with this place, Hector?"

"I built it. I fashioned everything you see. And I am not done yet. But come." He gestured toward a luxurious sofa. "Sit. Here we can speak freely about your father." Nicky Neill eased himself onto the couch. "Before we begin, may I bring you something to drink? Juice perhaps?"

"Water, Hector, please. I could really use some water."

Hector disappeared into the kitchen. When he returned he carried a large ceramic pitcher in one hand and a plate of tortillas in another.

"You are safe here, my friend. Eat, drink, and in time you will know all I know about your father. And I assure you I will assist you in any way I can."

Nicky Neill raised the pitcher to his lips with both hands. The cool water flowed down his parched throat and over his chin, splashing across his chest where it pooled gratefully in his lap.

"Ahhh," he gasped, setting the pitcher aside. "I can't thank you enough for that!" Nicky Neill wiped the liquid away from his upper lip and sighed a final time. "Okay, Don Hector, tell me all you know about Professor Carpenter."

CHAPTER 24

*H*ector settled into a chair across from the sofa. "Your father was captured by a Lacandon warrior patrol. I was told that he was walking down the old stone road near where you and your friend were first observed."

"My friend?" Nicky Neill interrupted. "Which friend would that be?"

"Why, the boy who escaped. The warriors were very frustrated that they could not find him. I am concerned that he will not survive the forest on his own."

"Hah! That boy knows his way around a jungle. His name's Jorge Campo. He's from Palenque. He'll find his way home, I'm sure of that. What more can you tell me about my father?"

"Right." Hector readjusted his position in the chair. "The warriors brought your papa into the village, where the priests interrogated him."

"Hold on," Nicky Neill signaled with a raised hand. "The old guys are priests? And they run everything?"

"Yes, yes, the priests are the elders. Mayan society was, and still is, a theocracy. In a theocracy the priests control everything. We are governed by a religious hierarchy..."

"A religious what?" Nicky Neill broke in again.

"A hierarchy," Hector explained. "This is a system of organization where power flows from the top. And here, the priests...all those old men, sit at the top. Now where was I?"

"Sorry, Hector. I want to understand everything. You were telling me about the priests interviewing my dad."

"Oh, of course!" Hector cleared his throat. "The warriors led your father before the senior priests. But in short order the professor caused a real hubbub."

"What do you mean? What did he do?"

"Well," Hector sighed, "he stirred things up. That's when I got interested. A crowd had gathered near the priests' quarters after they heard the old men wailing and arguing, something we don't hear much of around here. Anyway, I joined the mob and before long word leaked out that the white man inside spoke a fair bit of our language and, on top of that, he possessed an intolerable degree of knowledge concerning Lacandon history. But it was something else that really, uh, how do you say...riled the priests?"

"Riled, yeah, that's the word all right. What was it?" Nicky Neill sprang to his feet. "What did my dad do?"

"Please, my young friend," Hector motioned for his guest to retake his seat, "you must stay calm and concentrate. I myself do not fully understand this next part. You see, word slipped out that the white man had insight into Lacandon secret knowledge." Hector paused and studied the boy's face. "I have been here four years and never have I heard of such a thing, of secret knowledge."

"Oh, my! Leave it to my dad to know stuff he's not supposed to know...hmm. What does it mean, Hector? And what does secret knowledge have to do with where my dad is now?"

Hector stared at the floor, wrinkling and unwrinkling his brow. Then he looked up. "Well, though I don't understand the entire story, I can tell you this. For three days and nights, your papa stayed in the priests' residence. He was talking with the leaders the whole time. I saw food and drink go in, but the professor never came out. On the morning of the third day, the senior priests led your father outside. He was immediately surrounded by Jaguar Warriors; our fiercest fighters. Without fanfare, this group—your papa, the priests, and the warriors—proceeded to the river and crossed the forbidden bridge..."

"Wait!" Nicky Neill's legs unfolded and he sprang to his feet again. "Why is it called the forbidden bridge?"

"Because no one is allowed to cross it except for the priests, and even they seldom go there. One man, the high priest they call Xac-Mal, goes over it daily. He is the only one, really, who uses it."

"Well, dang, Hector! Where does this guy go when he uses the bridge?"

"He walks up the forbidden path and enters the door to Chultun Callí. Beyond that, I know nothing."

"Hector, you're talking in riddles! What is Chultun Callí? And is everything forbidden around here?"

"Patience, my young friend. This world has been ongoing for almost two thousand years; you cannot understand it in half an hour." Hector fell silent. The boy sank back onto the sofa and nodded his approval. "Very well," he continued. "As I was explaining, the priests, along with your papa and the Jaguar Warriors, continued across the forbidden bridge. Once across, the entire party made the ascent up the forbidden trail. But at the door to Chultun Callí, the procession stopped. Only your papa and Xac-Mal passed inside. I know all this because I hid by the river with my friend Kabal. We waited."

"What happened, Hector? How long did you wait? Did you see my dad come out again?"

When Hector next spoke he averted his gaze. Instead, he focused his attention on the floor. "We waited through midday. Still, no one reappeared at the door. My friend grew restless and returned to his home, but I stayed on. Finally, perhaps an hour or so before sunset, Xac-Mal stepped through the entrance. He was alone."

Nicky Neill's mouth fell open, but no words followed. He struggled to regain his voice.

"Solemnly," Hector continued, "Xac-Mal reunited with the group. He led them back down the path and over the bridge again. From there, they proceeded straight to the palace. They remained inside all through the night, with the warriors standing guard. Since that day, I have not seen or heard anything of your papa. That is almost a month now."

CHAPTER 25

"Whooooooo..." Every last breath of air emptied from Nicky Neill's lungs. He waited as long as he could before inhaling again. "So...Hector...what does this mean?"

Hector stared helplessly in his guest's direction.

"Okay, then. Tell me all you can about Chultun Callí. None of this will make sense until I understand what that place is."

"My friend," Hector's voice was heavy with uncertainty, "the door to Chultun Callí is a hole, an entrance. It is a passageway into the mountain itself. The mountain is Chultun Callí, and for the Lacandon it is sacred. For whatever reason, this is a holy place to them. All I know is that whatever secrets they possess, whatever ancient knowledge they have inherited, it is locked inside this mountain. What I am certain of," he hesitated, weighing his words, "is that only the high priests are privileged to know these things. Believe me, whatever secrets are kept in Chultun Callí cannot be known to outsiders. You will never get close to the door, my son. Ever."

Hector concluded his comments with such a strong tone of finality that Nicky Neill chose not to pursue the topic any further, but he had other pressing questions.

"Hector, how did you end up in this place, anyway?"

A broad smile spread across the man's face. "Ah, it was destiny, my friend. As I mentioned earlier, I was once a petroleum engineer. Four years ago I was in charge of an exploration team, inspecting this area for potential sampling sites. At the boundary of Lacandon territory, my crew refused to go any further. I berated them for being superstitious, for acting like children. They deserted me, on the spot. So I set off alone, with a minimum of equipment." He paused to laugh at himself. "I was hard-headed back then, and I was driven by the pursuit of profit. And that, my friend, is what drives the world."

Nicky Neill studied Hector. If there was one thing he had learned from this experience it was how to size adults up. Hector read like an open book. He was genuinely at peace with himself and this place.

"I carried on alone," he continued, "conducting my investigation. It was slow going. Two days later a warrior patrol surrounded me in the forest not far from the sacred temple. They brought me here. I was informed by other prisoners that I could never leave."

"That must have been awful," Nicky Neill interrupted. "Did you try to escape?"

"No," Hector replied matter-of-factly. "The punishment for attempted escape is death. I decided to become familiar with the place, learn all I could learn, before I took the risk. But as time passed, a funny thing happened."

"What was that?"

"I learned to like it here." A satisfied glow flushed across Hector's face. "I learned to love the peace in this forest, and I came to respect the Lacandon. As this attitude developed, I discovered something very exciting about myself."

"Uh-huh." Nicky Neill nodded. "What was that?"

"I learned I could do everything for myself. I learned complete independence. In my old life, when the water pipes broke or the sewage backed up, I threw my hands over my head in rage and frustration. I was powerless; there was nothing I could do. But here, I put my engineering skills to good purpose. I constructed my own water delivery system and shared it with the village. I also devised a sewage removal process that has greatly reduced the threat of disease. Oh, my son, I have done more, much more! As you can see, I built this house and everything in it with my own hands. I have made a list of things to accomplish and every day it grows! You understand, Nick, I am needed here.

These people do not value me for the wealth I have accumulated, or the profit I can bring them. No, they value me for the good I can do, for the ways I can enrich their lives." Hector paused and nodded reassuringly. "And I do these things with utmost respect for their culture, with no intent to change them or their way of life."

"Hector, you're one of the good guys..."

"Thank you, thank you. My life has meaning now, true meaning. I have entered this world and become a part of it. I no longer dream of escape. For me, the world outside this forest is a prison. I will never return there."

Hector ceased speaking. For a long moment, he remained motionless, staring into Nicky Neill's eyes.

"Hector," Nicky Neill spoke softly, "did you have a family before?"

"Huh? Oh, no, no! Not before. But I have a wife and small daughter now. They are away, visiting her family. You will meet them soon, I hope."

"Yes, sir. I look forward to that."

An easy silence fell over the two. Nicky Neill focused on Hector's story, but some pieces of it did not add up. Why, he wondered, would the Lacandon take his father into their holiest of places, into a mountain, and leave him there? Why Dad and not Hector? Something mysterious was going on and he was certain that he would have to come up with the answer himself. Then a thought dawned on him, a thought so awful, so hideous, it made his blood run cold.

"Hector," his voice struggled to push its way through his constricted throat, "I have to ask you something. And you must tell me the truth. Promise?"

"Yes, yes. Of course, my friend. Rest assured I will be truthful."

Nicky Neill's Adam's apple formed itself into a rock. He had to force his voice to work around it. "Do these...do the Lacandon...do these people still practice human sacrifice?"

Hector's eyes widened until they filled half his face. His breathing became faint, almost undetectable. His glowing complexion paled.

"Hector! Are you all right?" Nicky Neill reached out and placed a hand upon Hector's forearm. Still, he did not move. Finally, words slipped through his lips.

"I do not know, my son. I do not know the answer to that."

CHAPTER 26

$\mathcal{A}$s Nicky Neill and Hector wrestled with the emotions triggered by the latest topic in their conversation, a strange noise filtered through the walls of Hector's home.

"What's that?" Nicky Neill's voice continued to strain to clear the lump in his throat.

"A procession!" Hector exclaimed, springing to his feet. "Come! We must see what it is."

The pair hustled out the door of Hector's home and set off down the path toward the village. It wasn't long before they spotted a large crowd encircling a column of priests. In the midst of the wrinkled hierarchy, perched upon the shoulders of the fierce Jaguar Warriors, floated none other than Ploox. Trailing the procession, as always, the troupe of musicians ruptured the air with a strident joy.

"Where are they taking him?" Nicky Neill shouted above the din.

"To the pyramid, of course!" Hector yelled back. "Now that he is king, he must mark the passing of the sun each evening and its arrival each morning. From this time forward, he alone is responsible for the rising and setting of the life force. Its uninterrupted arrival and departure are proof of his favor with the gods."

"You mean the king is responsible for the sun coming up and going down? Holy cow, Hector! Do you believe that?"

"Certainly not. But the Lacandon do and that is all that matters. With the king's presence, the future of this world is assured ... of course, there are exceptions."

Nicky Neill clutched at Hector's elbow and reined him to a halt. "What do you mean, 'exceptions'?"

"Well, say we are plagued with a drought during the rainy season, or an unexplained crop failure. These things indicate displeasure from the gods, and the only way to regain their favor is by..." Hector's voice trailed off to a whisper as he turned away from his companion.

"Hector! Hector! How do they get back on the gods' good side?"

When Hector turned back to face the boy, he remained silent. From his expression, Nicky Neill could read his response. In that moment he had answered the awful question.

"Son, on a more positive note," Hector's features softened, "your friend has been given a new name. Do you know what the priests have christened him?"

"No, no sir. Ploox has a new name?"

"Ah, yes!" A broad smile flashed across Hector's face. "They call him Jaguar Comet...the king who fell from the sky!"

CHAPTER 27

$\mathcal{H}$ ector and Nicky Neill watched the procession until it faded from view. Rather than follow the parade, they returned to Hector's place. Hector ushered Nicky Neill inside, then excused himself to tend to his evening chores.

At first, the only thought Nicky Neill could muster was a take on the old refrain "out of the frying pan into the fire." Both his dad and Ploox were in a pickle. Know it or not, they were dependent on him to come through. He set the wheels in motion, and before long he crafted a plan.

That evening, Nicky Neill presented his scheme to Hector.

"Hector," he began, "do you keep any rope around your place?"

"Rope?" Hector rubbed at his chin. "Yes, I have rope...why do you ask?"

"Well, I've got a plan. I need at least twenty feet of strong rope and your help. Can I count on you?"

Hector pushed his plate away, planted his elbows on the table, and leaned toward his guest. "My young friend, I offer you the totality of my services. But, I must impose one condition."

"How do you mean, sir?"

"You must promise me that if you escape, you will do nothing to destroy this way of life."

Nicky Neill searched Hector's face. "Hmm, I get it. You mean like send in the army?"

"Yes, yes. Just that." With a pained expression he added, "Or worse yet, the U.S. Marines."

"There's no other place like this one that I know, Hector. For better or worse, I swear, I won't be the one to ruin it. You have my word no one will be seeking revenge on the Lacandon if we make it out of here."

"Thank you, my friend." Hector eased back into his chair. "Now, tell me about your plan."

"Well, it's not much of a plan, really, more like an angle to get me into that mountain. After that, I haven't a clue. Anyway, here it is. This spoon is the river at the base of the mountain. And this cup is the mountain. My idea is to climb up the backside tomorrow afternoon. I'll spend the night there. Come morning, you'll create a diversion, and while the guards are busy, I'll toss the rope off and shinny down. Then I'll sprint into the cave. With any luck, the guards won't notice the rope right away. What do you think?"

Hector shook his head. "This is not possible. It cannot work."

"Why is that, Hector?"

"The main reason, my brave friend, is simply because the mountain cannot be climbed. You see, the contours of the mountain were chiseled away long ago... the entire outer surface removed. A sheer rock wall remains in defiance of all who would consider scaling the peak. It is," he added, "a curious truth."

"Oh, my gosh!" Nicky Neill slumped down in his chair. "Someone trimmed a hunk of rock, an entire mountain! How is that possible?"

Hector could only shrug in response. But Nicky Neill could not let it go.

"How? I just can't make it right in my head! Native people, hundreds of years ago, people who didn't even have the wheel yet, lopped off the rough edges, including the jungle, of an entire mountain! Oh, man! I'm not sure we could pull that off today, with all the modern tools we have!" Nicky Neill shook his head in growing disbelief. "Hector, you're an engineer. Explain this to me."

A faint smile appeared on Hector's face. "I have no answer, my son. But I can offer you this much. The ancients were not ignorant beings, as modern man likes to believe. In fact, I tend to envision them as rather brilliant. How clever must they have been to sheer the exterior off a whole mountain without the benefit of dynamite, or giant drills, or motorized earth-moving equipment? Huh?"

"Wow! I never looked at it like that."

"Another thing, something else you likely did not know. The ancient Maya conceived of the concept of zero. That is a sublime, abstract accomplishment." Hector paused to allow the weight of his pronouncement to sink in. "Back to the present," he continued. "The mountain cannot be climbed. Gaining entrance to Chultun Callí is impossible. Simply impossible."

Just then the front door creaked sharply and swung open. At the same time, a voice echoed Hector's last word.

"Impossible? Please, sir! That word grates on my eardrums."

Hector and Nicky Neill snapped to attention, spinning hard on their chairs to face the doorway, mouths agape. The intruder stepped inside the dwelling and closed the door behind him.

CHAPTER 28

*T*he person who approached them was the biggest Lacandon Nicky Neill had encountered yet. He was dressed in the familiar white tunic, like Hector, and he wore similar leather sandals, but there was something odd about him. His thick, gray-black hair swept awkwardly over his face, making it difficult to get a clear look at him.

"No, sir," he spoke again, "impossible just ain't part of my vocabulary!"

The stranger continued to stare down at his bewildered audience. Then, with a swipe of his hand, he yanked the hair right off his head.

"One-Zero!" Nicky Neill popped to his feet. "How in the blazes did you get here?"

"Simple. I made myself a Lacandon and came home for supper!"

"One-Zero reveals himself"

74

"But the hair..." Nicky Neill eyeballed the long scalp in One-Zero's hand. "Please don't tell me Dr. Xama sacrificed that?"

"Not hardly, pardner," he laughed. "This headdress is a contribution from your horse's mane! Actually, from both horses!"

"Excuse me, señor. I am Hector Villaverde...and you?"

"Forgive me, sir. My name is One-Zero. This boy," he gestured toward Nicky Neill, "and your new king are friends of mine. I'm here to lend a hand...if requested, that is."

Hector rose and bowed. When he straightened up again, he extended his hand to One-Zero. "I am pleased to make your acquaintance. *Mi casa es su casa, señor.*"

One-Zero reached for Hector's hand and shook it warmly. "Don Hector, the pleasure is mine."

"Uh," Nicky Neill looked to Hector and then back to his friend, "One-Zero, would you care to join us?"

'Yes, do!" Hector seconded the offer. "And may I offer you stew and cornbread?"

"Armadillo stew is an old favorite of mine, an' I never turn down cornbread!" One-Zero pulled out a chair and eased himself onto it. "Ain't life grand!" he sighed.

Nicky Neill was quick to begin the questioning.

"One-Zero, what do you know about our predicament?"

"Well," he smiled broadly, dipping a wedge of cornbread into his stew bowl, "while I was hikin' with you boys, Helen was workin' on my outfit...you know, my costume. Soon as I got back I changed into my Lacandon self and set off for this place. And wouldn't you know it! First thing out of the box, I run into Jorge, crashin' through the forest like a rogue elephant!"

"Oh, man, thank goodness!" Nicky Neill crowed. "He made it!"

"Yep, he made it all right. That boy's got a lotta spunk. From the looks of him, he ran the whole way back. As you might imagine, he wanted to return with me. I sent him to the

75

house instead; he was due a rest. Later, he'll be guidin' the horses to a location by the river. Once he gets there, he'll set up camp and sit tight 'til he hears us comin'."

"Is he alone?" Nicky Neill grew anxious all over again.

"Naw, he ain't, not for the moment. Helen's with him. She'll keep him company for twenty-four hours, then she's got other chores to tend to."

"And what would those be?" Nicky Neill's shoulders relaxed.

One-Zero didn't respond right away. Instead, he focused on his meal. When the last piece of cornbread had sopped up the last speck of stew, he pushed his chair away from the table and looked first to Hector and then to Nicky Neill.

"Jorge is the last leg of our rescue effort. Now hear me out." One-Zero eased his elbows onto his knees. "After sendin' him off, I kept hikin' 'til I reached the village. Just in time, I might add, for the royal parade! My, Ploox cut a noble figure up there on those fellas' shoulders! When the crowd passed on, I set to surveying the area, getting a feel for the place. I've been here before, but on those occasions I was payin' attention to other things..."

Nicky Neill's expression registered surprise, but it faded quickly.

"Anyhow," One-Zero cleared his throat, "when I came back to the village, I spotted you two. I followed you here but I couldn't join you until I looked into a few more details. Glad I caught up to you fellas in time for supper!"

"Dang! One-Zero, how do you do all the things you do?"

One-Zero grinned back at the boy in response.

"The way I see it, there ain't a lot of time to waste. We have two jobs here: one is to find the professor and bring him back from wherever someone put him; the other is to spring Ploox before the charade breaks down. And," One-Zero looked his companions over closely, "we have to go about the task with Ploox in a very specific way."

"Could you elaborate, señor?" Hector asked.

"Hmm." One-Zero nodded. "We've got to liberate Ploox in a particular style so that the Lacandon see it as an omen, a work of the gods. These folks been plannin' on the king's return for hundreds of years...if he just runs out on them, or gets whisked away in a kidnapping, well, it'll do a heap of damage to this tribe. We have to avoid that."

"Oh, man," Nicky Neill straightened up in his chair, "I hadn't thought of any of that. This is way more complicated than I figured."

One-Zero leaned across the table and laid a hand on Nicky Neill's shoulder. "Everything is complicated, pard. But then, that's what these big things are for." He tapped his forehead with his free hand. "Our brains don't like to think, but when you put 'em to work, amazing things can happen!"

"You are a very wise man, señor," Hector added.

"So, how do we do it, One-Zero?" Nicky Neill's frustration was giving way to his curiosity. A fresh sense of possibility was in the air.

CHAPTER 29

O ne-Zero rocked back in his chair until the front legs were well off the floor. Then, ever so casually, he raised his legs to waist level and extended his arms outward on a plane with his shoulders. With that perpetual grin plastered across his face, One-Zero set his chair in motion. Nicky Neill and Hector watched as their friend "walked" the chair across the room to the fireplace, spun about, and returned to his original position.

"Hah!" He laughed out loud as the chair legs fell back to the floor.

"What the heck was that, One-Zero?" Nicky Neill joined in the laughter. "Have you done that before?"

"Naw," he continued, laughing, "first time for that trick."

Hector was smiling faintly, nodding his head in approval. "Señor One-Zero, everyone knows chairs have legs, but no one expects them to walk."

"Exactly, Hector, my friend. Exactly!"

One-Zero reached for the pitcher of water and filled his cup. After a long drink he looked his companions over.

"Okay, here's the scenario. Come mornin', Jorge will be staked out three miles downriver. His job is to sit tight, be invisible, stay at the ready, and keep a keen lookout for us. If we don't show up between sunrise and mid-mornin' the following day, then he's sworn to return to the tree house. And Jorge will go back to Palenque alone." One-Zero paused to allow that understanding to sink in. "Clock-wise, that gives us about thirty-seven hours to do our part."

"Why so little time, señor?" Hector inquired. "Why even place a time limit on such an undertaking?"

"Because that's all the time I reckon we'll need."

Hector glanced at Nicky Neill and each shrugged at the other.

One-Zero's gaze narrowed on Hector.

"As chief engineer of this territory, you've got a big chore ahead of you. Could be, Hector, that your part in all of this is the most difficult."

"My part? What am I to do, señor? What is my task?"

"It falls on you, my friend, to get Ploox out of that palace and down to the river bright and early, day after tomorrow."

One-Zero's explanation was issued so matter-of-factly that both Hector and Nicky Neill were caught off guard.

"Did I hear you correctly, señor?" Hector scooted closer to the table. "Did you say 'out of the palace'? Frankly, such a task is an imposs..." Hector cut his words short. "Forgive me," he continued. "What suggestions would you offer?"

"Well, you're gonna need one heck of a distraction to start with. And then," One-Zero cast a sly glance toward Nicky Neill, "let me ask you, Hector, what do you know about zip lines?"

Hector responded to One-Zero's query with a knowing smile. "Where will the king meet up with you?"

"Downstream a ways there's a big yellow tree. A cortez, right?"

Hector nodded in acknowledgment.

"At the base of that tree, or thereabouts, there's a canoe stashed. It's well hidden, so you'll have to trust me on this. Once you've located the boat, get Ploox to crawl underneath it and insist that he hide 'til we show up. And then you, sir, will slip back to the village and resume your life as an innocent party to all this."

"I see," Hector said. "But what remains unclear is how the priests will interpret the king's disappearance. How will they not see this action as a kidnapping? Or worse still, as an abdication?"

Nicky Neill looked to One-Zero. Had he overlooked this point? But his friend did not bat an eye.

"You're exactly right, Hector. That's why I have this." He reached under his tunic and withdrew a long leather pouch. Opening the flap, he pulled out a yellowed slip of paper. "This here," he waved the document about, "is a note for Ploox. These instructions spell out exactly what he should do and when to do it. And," he added, "the details will assist you with eliminating the evidence...the zip line in particular."

"Still," Hector persisted, "what about the king's disappearance? The priests will come for him at sunrise for the blessing at the temple. When they discover he is gone, chaos will surely follow."

"Again, you're spot-on, Hector. That's why we'll have to make use of this." He dug into the pouch again. This time he extracted a small white bag attached to a ball of odd-looking twine.

"What the heck is that?" Nicky Neill's brow furrowed deeply.

"Oh," One-Zero smiled, "the bag is filled with something that's a lot like gunpowder, and this string here," he twirled a strand between his fingers, "is pretty much a fuse."

"Can you spell it out for me, One-Zero?" Nicky Neill began to experience an uncomfortable sensation in his stomach.

"Okay, here's the short version. When Ploox is ready to zip off, he'll stick this string into the bag and trail the rest of it across the room. Then he'll put a match to it, which I've provided. When the powder blows, the second story will smolder a bit, long enough to encourage anybody down below to clear the palace. Then, once the bamboo ignites, a very short era will go up in a plume of fire and smoke."

"Holy cow, One-Zero! You sure all this will work?"

"Oh, I'm pretty certain, Nick, as long as we all do our parts."

Hector remained troubled. "Señor, how do I get this note and the other things into the hands of the king? And what of the zip line on his end? So many loose ends..."

The constant grin disappeared from One-Zero's face.

"Hector, loose ends is an apt metaphor for humankind. We're loose ends in a loose world, raveling and unraveling at the same time all the time. And yet, here we are!" The grin returned to his face. "I don't have answers for your questions, but I do know this. You'll work out the details just fine an' the plan will unravel as it should ... don't ya reckon?"

Hector looked first to Nicky Neill and then back to One-Zero. "It will be done," he said. "It will be done."

CHAPTER 30

While the responsibilities and urgency of One-Zero's plan soaked in, Nicky Neill was overcome with a burning desire for clarification.

"Hey, One-Zero. I have a few questions for you."

"Sure, pard. Shoot."

"You haven't been in the village all that long, have you?"

"That's right."

"Well, when did you find the time to put this complicated scheme together? I mean, the note to Ploox, the gunpowder, and the other stuff?" Nicky Neill shook his head in disbelief. "How'd you learn to think like this?"

One-Zero let loose a full-blown, gut-busting guffaw. He slapped his leg and dust exploded from his tunic.

"Son, when you've been around as long as I have, you learn to anticipate outcomes. When I spotted Ploox comin' out of that palace, I started calculatin' his escape. I wrote out that note not long after. Took me all of five minutes, maybe."

"And the gunpowder?"

"That I carry in my pouch, just in case, you know? Truth be told, I imagined we'd have to make use of it some other way!"

Hector and Nicky Neill looked at each other again, then back to One-Zero.

"So, what happens next? Do we bed down here and get started first thing in the morning?"

"No time to delay," One-Zero replied. "We've got a heap of ground to cover tonight."

"Tonight?" Nicky Neill feigned surprise. "Okay, what do we need to do?"

"We've got to get into that mountain sooner or later. I reckon tonight will be soon enough."

"What about me, señor?" Hector volunteered. "How can I help?"

One-Zero didn't miss a beat. "Sir, we'll need a candle, a couple of blankets, a container of water, and some dried meat. Is that a problem?"

"No, señor, I can provide all those things. ¿Con permiso?" He rose from his chair and went to work.

"How about me, One-Zero? Give me a job."

"What's become of your rucksack?"

"The Lacandon took it. Why?"

"Just wondering. A flashlight might come in handy...no problem though." He stopped talking and raised a finger toward the ceiling. "Come to think of it, reckon you could make a check outside, see that no one's spyin' on us?"

"Yes, sir." Nicky Neill crept to the doorway, cracked it apart, and slipped through the opening. Outside, he melted into the darkness. For a minute he remained still, listening and adjusting his eyes to the night. Then he eased into the bush and proceeded to circle Hector's home. When he felt confident they were not being observed, he made his way back to the dwelling and eased himself inside again. At that moment, Hector was passing a bag and a stack of blankets to One-Zero.

"Thank you, Don Hector." One-Zero squeezed the man's arm as he accepted the provisions. "We appreciate your help and your hospitality. I promise you, your life will get back to normal when this is over."

"Yes," Hector smiled, "that will be nice. To be truthful, I have been troubled since Nicky Neill's father first appeared. When he disappeared I sensed a foreboding that I have not experienced in all my years with the Lacandon." Hector paused to gather his thoughts. "Now, with our new king, I find myself even more alarmed. I cannot explain these feelings. Ours is a fragile world; I think you know this. It would not take much to upset the balance and tear the Lacandon way of life apart."

One-Zero nodded and locked eyes with the petroleum engineer. "Have a good life, Don Hector. And a long one! Nicky Neill, are you ready and willing?"

"Yes, sir."

"Good. One final thing." One-Zero peeled off his white tunic and draped it over a chair. Nicky Neill was not surprised to see his friend wearing his pants with the legs rolled up. Tucked inside his pants was a dark shirt. "Hector, see to it that Ploox ... pardon me, the king, leaves his royal clothes behind when he ducks out of here, okay? If the Lacandon do catch a glimpse of him in the course of the escape, it would be better he not appear too kingly! I reckon this tunic will fit His Majesty."

"I will see to it," Hector promised.

"We're off then." One-Zero headed for the door.

Nicky Neill turned to Hector. "I've only known you a short while, but in that time you've been a great help. And you've become a true friend. Thank you, Hector. I'll never forget you." Nicky Neill extended his hand. But Hector did not take it. Instead he pulled the boy close and hugged him.

"Nor shall I forget you, my son. Go with God, and all will be well. Adios."

"Adios." Nicky Neill spun about and followed One-Zero out the open doorway. The sliver of light that bathed their exit shrank to a pinpoint, then disappeared with a click as the door sealed shut behind them.

CHAPTER 31

O utside again, Nicky Neill was struck blind by the darkness a second time. He imagined One-Zero was adjusting to the murky pitch as well, but he could not see or hear anything of his friend.

"Hey!" he whispered. "Where are you?"

"Straight ahead."

Soon Nicky Neill's hands were groping One-Zero's back.

"Ah, okay...there you are! What's our next move?"

"Well," he spoke softly over his shoulder, "we'll take it slow and easy and mosey our way down to the bridge."

"You mean the forbidden one? Hector said there are guards all over it."

"We have to start somewhere. That bridge will make some decisions for us. Besides, I always was curious 'bout forbidden stuff. C'mon, I can almost see."

Nicky Neill stuck as close to One-Zero as possible, which meant he kept a firm grip on his friend's shirttail. He remained hard-pressed to see his own hand in front of his face. His two-hundred-year-old guide, however, seemed to know exactly where he was going.

They made their way through the sleeping village and on to the far side where the earth sloped sharply down to the river. When they reached the water's edge, their pace slowed to a crawl. One-Zero eventually parted the brush and gestured toward some fixed point in the shadows.

"There." He drew Nicky Neill alongside him. "The bridge is twenty meters ahead...can you make it out?"

"All I see is black, and more black on top of that. How do you know there's a bridge there?"

"Don't look directly at it, son. Scan, sweep your eyes back and forth, slowly. You want an image to emerge. You won't see a bridge, per se, rather a shape. Try it."

Nicky Neill did as instructed. Sure enough, a dark form materialized each time his gaze moved across the void.

"Yeah, yeah, I see it. At least, I see something. If you say it's a bridge, then I'm with you. What now?"

"Ever see a blowgun work?"

Before Nicky Neill could comment, One-Zero began probing into his long leather pouch. Soon, he was screwing something together. Then he pried the lid off a container and withdrew several objects.

"Give me your hand, Nick. These are darts. Don't touch the tips, or you'll be sleeping for the next four hours."

Nicky Neill accepted a small bundle of slender reeds on his palm, closing his fingers to secure them in place. He had no idea which end of the darts was which.

"Hold your breath, pard. We'll see if I still got the touch."

Nicky Neill remained motionless while One-Zero slipped a dart into his device. "Here goes," he whispered. He inhaled deeply and brought the instrument to his mouth. A burst of air surged through his lips. *Whooo-whew!* Then all was quiet again.

Nicky Neill waited anxiously, but nothing happened.

"Well?" He nudged his companion. "What's supposed to..."

Ker-thump. A dull thud resounded on the night air.

"Patience, pardner." One-Zero rose to a crouching position. "Some things take time, don't ya know?"

Nicky Neill unfolded himself from his squatting position and tiptoed after his accomplice, who was now moving forward more quickly than before. He still couldn't see much, but new shapes had begun to form in his field of vision.

"Here you are," One-Zero addressed the shadows as he reached out and touched something firm. "Give me your hand, Nick." His voice was low, beneath a whisper. Nicky Neill extended his right arm and One-Zero grasped his wrist, guiding it forward.

"Whoa!" Nicky Neill hissed under his breath. "It's a body! Is he dead?"

"Dead to the world," One-Zero replied. "But it ain't a permanent condition. In a couple of hours he'll come around an' wonder what coconut put his lights out."

One-Zero moved closer to his victim and ran his hands over the man's body.

"Ah, there you are." Showing considerable care, he extracted the dart from its resting place. "No need to leave a calling card, huh."

"Now what?" Nicky Neill's voice trembled with excitement.

"We relax and locate our next target."

One-Zero slid the used dart back into his pouch. When he looked up, Nicky Neill stood ready with a fresh projectile. Once it was loaded, the two stepped around the fallen guard and moved toward the bridge.

A new wave of adrenaline coursed through Nicky Neill's body. He feared the bridge would creak beneath their combined weight. He feared the guard would regain consciousness. He feared a booby trap would activate and ventilate every square inch of his body. But the soothing gurgle of fast-running water beneath his feet obscured what little noise they made and calmed his nerves.

In a matter of seconds the pair reached the far side of the span. One-Zero gently collapsed upon the path and began to crawl, lizard-like, up the forbidden trail. Nicky Neill followed suit.

The pair slithered forward for several minutes until a sound ahead of them arrested their movement. The noise repeated itself. It was a cough.

"Okay," One-Zero murmured, twisting sideways to address Nicky Neill's ear. "Let's hope we find another lone ranger at this end, too."

After a momentary pause, the two set off again, only at an even slower pace than before. Nicky Neill grew alarmed that the sound of their breathing would draw attention to them. Seconds ticked off like minutes on an invisible clock. Then they came face-to-face with the very guard they were stalking. The unexpected confrontation startled all parties equally. The warrior, however, was more surprised than the trespassers. For a split second, Nicky Neill made out the man's silhouette poised in alarm while his mind calculated his next move. In that instant, One-Zero beat him to the draw.

Whooo-whew! signaled the flight of the dart. In what seemed the same instant, One-Zero bound upward and slapped a hand over the guard's mouth. Although the man was stunned, his right arm arched backward, his spear tip poised to drive into One-Zero's neck.

Nicky Neill lunged at the warrior's legs, driving him to the ground. His spear crashed into the dirt behind them.

"Nice tackle, pard! You just saved the game." One-Zero patted Nicky Neill's shoulder as he rose to his feet. "Unfortunately, we have a problem here...what to do with our friend."

"Will he remember us when he comes to?"

"Precisely. My concoction knocks 'em out; it don't erase their memories."

"So, what's your idea?"

One-Zero didn't answer right away.

"Okay," he finally announced. "We'll take him with us!"

"With us?" Nicky Neill struggled to control his voice. "You've got to be kidding?"

One-Zero ignored the boy's comment. Rather, he busied himself ripping the guard's tunic into strips, which he then used to bind the man's wrists and ankles. The last of the garment was employed as a gag and a blindfold. That accomplished, One-Zero hoisted the unconscious figure into the air and slung him over his shoulder.

"Aaah!" He turned to Nicky Neill. "Let's get into that cave before this mission turns into a party!"

CHAPTER 32

$\mathcal{N}$ icky Neill wanted to protest, but he could not come up with any alternatives to One-Zero's decision. They had to bring the guard. A burst of bad-ending scenarios flashed before his eyes and caused his heart to race. His descent into despair was interrupted as the trio passed into another world. An additional blanket of darkness fell over them, followed by a breath-stealing chill.

"Little brother!" One-Zero called out. "Are you behind me?"

"Yeah. What just happened?"

"Catch up, pard, an' take hold of my shirt. Whatever you do, don't let go, an' don't get separated. We're in the mountain now."

"One-Zero leads Nicky Neill deeper into the darkness of the forbidden cavern"

One-Zero stopped moving and crouched to the floor. He began fumbling about with his free hand. After a moment, there was a rasping sound upon the stone beneath their feet, followed by a blinding flash as a match head crackled into flame. One-Zero lit Hector's candle and extinguished the match, taking care to deposit it in his bag.

"So," he turned to face Nicky Neill, "we're in the forbidden cavern, where no white man has ever tread before...except," he added, "quite likely your dad. How's it suit ya?"

"Gawwh!" was all Nicky Neill could muster. One-Zero fell silent as well. Words were not adequate for the forbidden world.

The two searchers and their unconscious companion found themselves in the outermost portion of an enormous chamber. Every shadowy boundary their light touched upon yielded larger-than-life, fantastically hideous figures that sprang from the walls as if released by the candle's blaze. The images were sculpted from the raw stone of the cavern. Each statue was so mysterious that Nicky Neill could not look away. He struggled to fathom their meaning. The figures were in a class to themselves, half men, half monster, part serpent or jaguar, occupants of some long ago sculptor's nightmare.

"What the heck, One-Zero...what is this place?" Nicky Neill's fingers doubled their hold on his friend's shirttail.

"Vestibule." One-Zero's voice was faint. "We're in the parlor now."

"Huh? What do you mean?" But One-Zero did not respond. "One-Zero! I'm worried about a warrior patrol looking for a missing sentry. They'll be climbing all over our butts any second!"

"Oh! Right, pard. Right you are. The Lacandon..." He rose from his crouching position and began moving cautiously to his left.

"Where are you going?" Nicky Neill asked.

"Got to drop off our passenger. This way ought to do it." One-Zero continued shuffling.

They traveled thirty paces before they encountered a serious dilemma. The blackness ahead of them yielded to the candle's light, revealing five separate passageways, each one branching off in a distinct direction.

"For crying out loud!" Nicky Neill muttered. "This is crazy!"

"It's supposed to be." One-Zero turned to his companion. "Actually, the purpose is to confuse."

"You mean you know about this?"

"Uh-huh. Translated from the original Mayan glyphs on the wall back there, more than eight hundred years old by the way, this area is called the Five Gates of Deception. Three of the passages lead to abrupt drop-offs, which, allegedly, empty into the underworld. A fourth tunnel leads to an underground corridor that snakes through the strata and comes up somewhere in the present-day ruins of Palenque."

"You mean the town of Palenque?"

"No, not the town. I mean the ruins, the site that once served as the spiritual center for all Mayaland. You boys passed not far from it on your way to find me. It's an extraordinary place and rumor has it that a subterranean passageway existed between Palenque and this mountain. I reckon if it's so, then one of these openings would likely be that route. But that's not of interest to us now."

"So, what is the fifth hole?"

"Darned if I know. That one's a mystery."

"You going to toss a coin here, One-Zero?"

"Hah, that's the spirit. But first things first." One-Zero eased the senseless guard off his shoulder. "This is your stop, amigo," he joked. "Take the candle, Nick. I want to be sure this fella can sit upright until help comes."

Nicky Neill held the candle and shed light while One-Zero positioned the Mayan into a semi-sitting position against the tunnel wall.

"Okay, that'll do." One-Zero straightened out to his full height. "Lead us back to the big hall, pard, and we'll pick our destiny."

With the guard out of the picture, Nicky Neill felt a rush of confidence. But when they reached their former post in the antechamber and squared off in front of the Five Gates of Deception, it began to fade. It was impossible to know which passage to take. He passed the candle to One-Zero. "We're stuck. We've got a one in five chance of getting this right...dang!"

"Cheer up, Nick! Those aren't bad odds, not bad at all. You may have the answer to all of this and not even know it."

"Huh? What are you saying?"

"I want you to relax a minute, close your eyes, and tell me everything Hector told you about this place."

Nicky Neill closed his eyes, wrinkled his brow, and squinted into his memory. "Here's all I remember." For the next two minutes he related the condensed version of the story Hector had shared with him about his life with the Lacandon, concluding with the witnessing of his dad being led away to their present location by Xac-Mal. When he finished his account, he opened his eyes. One-Zero was looking right at him. "Well, what did you get out of that?" The tone of Nicky Neill's voice lacked any shred of confidence.

"Hector said that Xac-Mal enters the cave every day, does he?" One-Zero asked.

"Yes, sir. That's what he told me. What of it? Are we going to wait for him to stroll in come morning?"

"What that means is that a pair of feet come and go across this floor every day. No doubt, a high priest has made this same trip, just like ol' Xac-Mal, for the last six or seven hundred years. Now, Nick," One-Zero placed a hand on the boy's shoulder, "stone may be stone, but time and flesh do have their effect."

"Run that by me again, One-Zero. You lost me!"

"No time." He laughed. "You'll just have to get the feel of it!" With that, he blew out the candle and the icy arms of darkness embraced them again.

CHAPTER 33

"Agghh!" Nicky Neill shrieked like a toddler tumbling off a stair step. "Jeepers, One-Zero, are you nuts?"

"Oh, I forgot my prize distraction," he muttered. "Hold your candle out again."

"Sure, no problem." Nicky Neill lifted the candlestick and pointed it in the direction of One-Zero's voice.

Prrr-rip! A match head raced over the cave floor and burst into flame. One-Zero lit the wick and dropped the still-smoldering splinter into his pouch.

"I think you'll like this." He plunged a hand back into his bottomless satchel and began fishing about. While his fingers flew, his gaze darted to the nearby walls. "Ah, there! That ledge will do just fine. Follow me over."

Nicky Neill trailed after, making sure to keep the flame alive. His trembling hand was no help.

"Look at this!" One-Zero flashed a shiny silver object under his companion's nose.

"Wow! What is it? It looks old."

"This is a Spanish amulet fashioned in pure silver. I figure it was crafted somewhere around the seventeenth or eighteenth century. Catches your eye, don't it?"

"Man-oh-man, One-Zero! Where did you get that? Don't tell me you picked it up off the floor!"

"No, sir, I uncovered it in some ruins over in the Yucatan a while back. Right now, I'm hopin' to boggle a few minds when that search party swoops down on our trail."

"Oh, I get it. At least, I think I do. The Lacandon will figure the Spaniards are back...ho-leee! They'll think the conquistadores have returned! One-Zero, this might really stir them up!"

"Yeah, somethin' like that."

When he reached the wall, he rose up on his tiptoes and positioned the amulet upon a small outcropping of rock.

"They oughta see that, huh?" He backed away from the wall into the center of the chamber. The object gleamed in the faint light. "Like a star in the heavens, I reckon!"

"Now what?" Nicky Neill reached out and refastened his grip on One-Zero's shirttail. Then he braced himself.

"Back to black." One-Zero puffed out the candle a second time.

"I give up, One-Zero. What is it we're about to do?"

"Ol' Xac-Mal strolls into the cavern every day, right? And whatever it is he does, it's my hunch he does it over and over. I suppose he performs a ritual of some sort. Anyway, our chore is to find his footsteps and follow 'em."

"That's the plan? In the dark?" Nicky Neill couldn't believe his ears. "Wouldn't candlelight at least show up the dust from his sandals?"

"It ain't tracks we want, exactly. It's the worn-down trail in the stone we're after."

"Ahh! I get it." Nicky Neill jammed the candle into his back pocket and dropped down to his hands and knees. His friend was already on all fours.

"Think about what we're doing," One-Zero whispered. "Imagine that old priest's feet shufflin' over this floor, day in, day out. Ease your mind down to your fingertips and concentrate...concentrate."

Nicky Neill did as he was instructed. At first, all he could feel was cold stone and the roughness and irregularities of natural rock. But he gradually began to detect subtle differences upon the surface.

"One-Zero! Here! I think I'm on to something. Feel it, under my hand."

One-Zero stopped sweeping and sidled next to Nicky Neill. He slid his palms beneath his companion's. Both of them stopped breathing.

"That's it, pard! You're on to it, all right. You take the lead. But remember, easy does it. Stretch those arms as far as you can before you let your body follow." He lifted his hand and placed it upon the boy's shoulder. "If you dive into the underworld, there's no comin' back!"

Nicky Neill swallowed hard and focused on the task. He knew he had to both relax and concentrate. With that in mind, he set out in pursuit of Xac-Mal's trail, with both hands leading the way. One-Zero brought up the rear, his right hand knotted in his guide's shirttail.

CHAPTER 34

$\mathcal{N}$icky Neill followed the infinitesimal depressions in the stone with a certainty that astounded him. The pair inched over the cold rock until their knees ached and the muscles in their backs throbbed. On and on they labored, winding left then right, and always down, deeper into the heart of the forbidden mountain.

Although Nicky Neill remained in the lead, he could feel One-Zero behind him, double-checking their course. And then, out of the blue, the trail vanished.

"Hold up! Hold up! I lost it! It's gone!"

"Whoa, now." One-Zero edged in beside him. "It can't just evaporate, we know that. Allow me to tickle the stone a bit. I don't have your touch, but I might pick up on something different, ya know?"

Nicky Neill scooted aside. One-Zero caressed the stone in a 360-degree pivot. When he ceased moving he was facing the near wall of the tunnel.

"Well, I'll be," he declared as he came to his feet.

"What?" Nicky Neill whispered. "What did you find?"

"Give me your paw, pard." Nicky Neill edged closer to his companion and extended his arm. One-Zero grasped his hand and pressed it against the glassy surface of the wall.

"Well," Nicky Neill demanded, "now what?"

"Explore it!" One-Zero laughed. "Tell me what you find."

With renewed concentration, Nicky Neill began to run his open hand over the stone, searching for an unexpected clue. Again and again he skimmed the area, but nothing came of it.

"Okay," he sighed in frustration. "I give up. What did I miss?"

"Don't feel bad, Nick. It's not the kind of surprise you can anticipate. What we're faced with here is a door!"

"Hah! If there's a door on this danged wall, I'll have a heck of a time getting through it!"

"Believe me, it's a door, all right. Indian stonemasons were a talented bunch...you'll have to visit Peru one day to admire what the Incas did with their rock. Anyway, this is where we wait." One-Zero sighed. "We'll need to locate a comfy spot where we can lay low. I reckon Mr. Xac-Mal has got a key to that door."

Before Nicky Neill could pose a question, One-Zero had a match lit. Once the boy's eyes adjusted to the intensity of the yellow flame, he made a careful study of the wall where One-Zero had discovered "the door." Try as he may, he could not detect a single crack or line in the stone that hinted at an opening.

"Look there, One-Zero!" Nicky Neill pointed down the tunnel at the opposite wall. "Is that ledge big enough for the two of us?"

"Good eye, son! I do believe that's the perch for us." In that instant, One-Zero blew the match out before it scorched his fingers. "We can't afford another match; the smell will give us away. Let's move to the ledge."

The pair inched across the tunnel to the far wall and groped their way to the outcropping. When they reached their nesting spot, One-Zero boosted Nicky Neill onto the overhang. Then he passed along their blankets and Hector's satchel of provisions before he pulled himself up and eased into position.

"A berth!" He chuckled. "This mattress is a tad firmer than what I'm used to, but it'll do! So, let's eat. Then we'll see how much rest we can get before the fireworks start."

Nicky Neill broke out the dried meat and water. He was pleased to discover that Hector had thrown in some bananas as well. He was famished. When chow was over, One-Zero offered some unsettling instructions.

"Okay, that was sweet but way too brief! Back to work, huh? Nick, wrap yourself up tight in your blanket, and be sure to cover your head."

"Why should I do that? Are you afraid a bolt of sunlight will flood in here and interrupt my nap?"

"Nice humor." One-Zero laughed. "I was thinking more of the bats."

"Bats! What bats? I haven't seen any bats in here at all."

"Oh, they're in here, all right. And those little vampires are known to carry rabies. So keep your noggin covered. No need to advertise. In the meantime, get some shut-eye. There's nothing more for us to do."

With One-Zero's encouraging advice, Nicky Neill pulled the blanket over his head and made sure the rest of his aching body was tucked into his protective envelope. Without realizing it, he drifted into a deep sleep.

CHAPTER 35

When Nicky Neill became conscious again, it was because One-Zero's hand was clamped over his mouth and one of his knees was bouncing against his rib cage. He tried to speak but that proved impossible, so he tapped One-Zero's arm to signal he was awake. With that, One-Zero drew closer and whispered in his ear.

"Don't move. Don't talk. We've got company. When I nudge you, poke your head out and look towards the door."

One-Zero removed his hand from Nicky Neill's mouth. As instructed, his partner played opossum. While he laid there, heart pounding, he strained to grasp the situation.

A brittle, ancient-sounding voice chanted in the near distance. As seconds ticked away, Nicky Neill recognized the language. It was the old Mayan tongue that the Lacandon priests used in their rituals. The voice, droning on and on, belonged to Xac-Mal. What the boy heard was eerie, like eavesdropping through a crack in time, listening to something from a long-forgotten era of human history.

Then, One-Zero nudged him. He stripped the blanket from his head and twisted his torso in the direction of the commotion. The chanting had reached the level of a shout.

The passageway was bathed in an amber glow. A small pot rested on the cave floor, spouting a gently undulating flame and a steady plume of sweet-smelling smoke. Xac-Mal stood before the wall where One-Zero had detected a door. His arms were in earnest supplication, invoking the stone to do who-knew-what. Nicky Neill experienced an intense urge to fly off his hiding place and grab the old man by the throat and make him cough up what he knew about his dad. Instead, he focused on the priest, who was practically braying at that point.

Xac-Mal was distinct from the others of his kind. He did not appear quite so gaudy in his attire. Gold and jade adorned his robe, but in a subdued fashion. In the amber light, his body shimmered and the effect was mirage-like. His headdress, a hood of quetzal feathers, added an iridescent, kaleidoscopic quality that further heightened the phantom impression. From the knees down, feathered leggings contributed to the notion that he wavered in and out of time itself. He was easy to stare at. The strongest sensation he invoked was one of authority and power.

Without warning, the chanting ceased. A heavy silence permeated the tunnel. Then it began.

Kkkrrrrrr-uurrk! A long, abrasive creaking noise erupted from the opposite wall. Nicky Neill cocked his head and listened, trying to pinpoint the origin of the clatter. In a split second he determined it was coming from the section of wall directly in front of Xac-Mal.

A thin wedge of white light broke loose from the stone and shot across the corridor. Nicky Neill's mind reeled from the shock of what he observed. Before he could recover from his astonishment, the dazzling curtain of light doubled, tripled, quadrupled itself in breadth and intensity. Then an enormous section of stone separated from the solid rock and swept out toward the high priest.

"One-Zero!" Nicky Neill mouthed the words beneath his breath.

"That's right, pard. There's our door."

CHAPTER 36

*I*n complete and utter fascination, Nicky Neill watched the monstrous slab of stone pull apart from the mountainside and swing into the corridor. The noise was almost unbearable, like an army of fingernails scraping across an endless chalkboard.

Then all movement below ceased. A veil of dust and debris quivered in the dazzling sunlight. The door itself almost filled the tunnel behind the priest.

Xac-Mal knelt on the cave floor, facing the gaping hole he had seemingly created. He was bowing so low that his quetzal headdress kissed the stone each time he bent over.

Whatever, or whomever, he was submitting to must have been a powerful force because the old priest appeared as humble as a schoolboy cowering before the paddle.

Seconds ticked by. Xac-Mal stopped bowing and slowly made his way back to his feet. Then he began speaking.

"What's he talking about, One-Zero?" Nicky Neill whispered behind cupped hands.

"Can't tell for sure, but I'll wager it has to do with us."

Just then, excited shouting erupted up tunnel. Xac-Mal stopped talking and backed into the center of the corridor to listen.

"Uh-oh! They found the amulet."

"How do you know?" Nicky Neill asked.

"Because they're hollerin' 'bout the Spaniards and a fella called Cortez."

Xac-Mal relayed what he had heard to whomever was on the other side of the doorway. His arms fluttered wildly over his head as he spoke. Then he spun about on his heels and took off running in the direction of the excitement, shrieking as he squeezed around the slab of stone that obstructed his path.

"Where's he going, One-Zero? Why don't those guys come down here?"

"Oh, I imagine they're not allowed. As a matter of fact, I reckon they..." One-Zero stopped whispering. His body tensed. His gaze riveted on the opening.

"What's wrong?" Nicky Neill shifted his attention back to the gaping hole that continued to bleed sunlight and dust into the darkness. What he saw next altered his understanding of the world.

CHAPTER 37

Golden sunlight flooded through the breach in the wall. As Nicky Neill gaped at the smoldering passageway, a dark shadow appeared, followed by the outline of a person. Framed in the river of sunshine, the individual was difficult to make out. When he stepped deeper into the tunnel, however, he became fully visible. Were it not for the sudden thrust of One-Zero's hand over his mouth, Nicky Neill would have cried out in uncontainable terror.

As he continued to marvel at the figure, he recalled a painting of just such a man in one of the books he had pored over at Ace's place. The scene in the book depicted a ritual. Tightly bound prisoners of war were being subjected to a hideous sacrifice. The presiding figure in that gruesome drama was like the man before them now, a lord or high priest, maybe a sorcerer. He held the power of life and death and wielded it for all to see.

The man who had stepped into the tunnel was not from the present. He was, in some unexplainable way, a projection from another time, an era stretching back into the past hundreds, if not thousands, of years. The figure exuded superiority and supreme confidence. Lying there on that dark shelf, Nicky Neill began to fear that they would be detected, that suddenly the guy would just know they were there and that his wrath would be terrible. The boy's breathing grew fainter. He imagined his body melting into the pores of the rock.

Like Xac-Mal, the man who straddled the passageway was dressed in splendid attire. But the quality of his garments surpassed the garb worn by the old Lacandon. This individual was cloaked in a jaguar skin cape that stretched to the floor and trailed after him. The edges of the cape glistened and shimmered in the sunlight, reflecting back a brighter gold than the sun's rays themselves. His arms and legs were adorned with jewelry, while the leather bindings on his sandals disappeared beneath thick jade plates secured above his kneecaps. In one hand he clutched a staff with a jaguar head at the top, a sculpture that appeared to be made of solid gold. His other hand was hidden by a furl of his cape.

The figure remained motionless, poised in the opening. His attention was focused up-tunnel where Xac-Mal had disappeared. He stepped forward two paces and peered down-tunnel where the trespassers were hiding. For the first time, his face was exposed.

The man's forehead swept back at an unnatural angle while his nose angled forward like a small banana. At the tip, a jade cylinder protruded through the partition between his nostrils, jutting out at either side. A wide jade collar rested on his neck and shoulders. More jade, in the form of beads and square chunks, dangled low from his earlobes. With a slight twitch of his head, his eyes became visible, and Nicky Neill recoiled in horror as they swept from side to side, scanning the darkness. His gaze was fierce and menacing. A faint shade of orange smoldered from the back of deep-set sockets.

Real fear attacked Nicky Neill's brain. For the first and only time of their travels, he wished they had stayed home.

Part II

Lost World

CHAPTER 38

*F*renzied shouting erupted up-tunnel again. The fearsome person in the doorway took a step backward. After a brief hesitation, he launched himself in the direction of the noise.

"Come on!" One-Zero elbowed Nicky Neill. "Now's our chance."

"Huh?" Nicky Neill watched as One-Zero rolled off the ledge, dragging his blanket and bag of provisions with him.

"Move, pard!" One-Zero's feet echoed off the stone floor. "Now!" In a heartbeat, he dashed through the sunlit opening and was gone.

Nicky Neill's paralysis melted in the greater fear of being alone in a cave filled with swelling numbers of Mayan hornets. He skittered off his perch and sprinted across the tunnel and through the opening before his own shadow knew he was gone. His blanket trailed after him, shedding small winged rodents as he flew.

Some eight or ten feet beyond the doorway, Nicky Neill skidded to a stop. He was blinded by the raging glare of the morning sun. A new panic seized him.

"One-Zero! Where are you?"

"To your left, Nick. Over here."

Nicky Neill kept his head low and side-shuffled in the direction of the voice. He still could not see One-Zero, but he managed to make out a cluster of huge boulders strewn about the earth in his path. Somewhere in that slew of rock was his friend.

"Cover your eyes, pard, and look up!"

Nicky Neill pulled his blanket over his shoulders and stretched it forward, creating an effective sunscreen. One-Zero's head popped into view between a pair of giant marbles.

"Sorry, man, I didn't mean to leave you so far behind. You've got to have a look at this." He waved Nicky Neill over and promptly disappeared again.

When the boy reached the stone spheres, he dropped to his knees and crawled through the crack at their base. On the other side he spied One-Zero crouched low beside an unearthly contraption.

"Man-oh-man! What in the Howdy Doody is THAT thing?" He stood up slowly and moved beside his friend.

"I've seen a few sights in my time. But this," One-Zero exhaled in admiration, "is a doozy!"

It was obvious to Nicky Neill that what they confronted was man-made. Beyond that, it was a riddle.

The entire contraption rested on a thick stone slab, ten feet in length and a yard wide. It was easily a foot thick. At either end of the slab, squat pedestals of jet-black rock protruded upward two feet. The top of each pedestal bore a deep groove. Each groove cupped an enormous skull-shaped crystal. Looking directly at the crystals proved difficult. Nicky Neill had never seen anything so beautiful and yet alarming at the same time. The crystals were six feet from top to bottom, and a good two feet thick at their center. Oddly, the morning sun did not reflect off them. What made them all the more difficult to admire was the sense that they were dangerous beyond appearance. Between the skull crystals a strange stone pillar rose to a height of four feet. The pillar was covered with carvings of detailed inscriptions and glyphs. At this point the device became even more puzzling. A thin platform of crude metal rested on top of the pillar and a pair of half-moon-like, translucent discs sprouted from the platform itself. Angling away from each disc, tethered to the base of the corresponding black pedestal, were two bloodred mirrors seemingly floating in place.

"What...what is this thing?" Nicky Neill could not pull his eyes away from the device. At the same time, a small but clear voice in his head was urging him to run.

One-Zero rose to his full height and glanced over his shoulder toward the hole that still gaped in the mountainside. "My guess is that this gizmo is a counter-crystal image stabilizer."

"Say what?"

"Yeah, I know." One-Zero shrugged. "Hear me out." He lowered himself into a squatting position again. Nicky Neill followed suit. "Right this minute, we're in a hidden place, and a fair-sized place it is, too. From where we are, you can't see out and the outside world can't see in. That means that for whoever lives here, the rest of the world doesn't exist. And likewise, this place doesn't exist anywhere else outside of this mountain."

"What about airplanes? Couldn't anyone flying over get an eyeful?"

"Good point. An' that's where this thing comes in." One-Zero motioned to the apparatus before them. "When aircraft fly over this part of the country, what they see is exactly what we're seeing now when we look up: sky and clouds. From this location we might hear an airplane but we wouldn't see it."

"Defying imagination Mayan ingenuity results in truly magical camouflage"

"Whoa, I still don't follow you."

"This gadget reflects a perfect image of the sky exactly as it was the day they set it up."

"Huh? Are you saying this is a camera?"

"Hmm, try this. Your notion of a camera is spot-on. Imagine this contraption recorded the way the sky looked at the moment it was activated. The nature of this beast is to bounce that picture back up in the air and then right back down here again, and so on, as long as it remains operational. The result is that whenever anyone looks up, way up, they see the same sky without variation." One-Zero paused to chuckle. "I wager there's a number of these doo-dahs scattered around the valley and they all work in tandem to reflect the same image. In other words, these things maintain a shield that prevents the outside world from lookin' in and the inside world from seein' out."

"Sure," Nicky Neill nodded, "it's a barrier. And it's a time machine as well. I don't have a clue how it works, but I understand what it's doing. You know, Hector said that modern people like to peg ancient folks as primitive. I'm not so sure about that anymore."

One-Zero continued to admire the machine. "Primitive," he replied softly. "That concept is open to interpretation, don't ya know?"

"Have you ever seen anything like this before?" Nicky Neill asked.

"Hmm, not exactly like this. But I have seen other variations."

"Hold on, now! Where else did you see them? How many are there?"

"Word is, seven secret places exist in the world. This is one. I've observed two others." He turned to face Nicky Neill. "Once you know a place like this, your view of the world will never be the same."

"Heck, One-Zero, no need to tell me that. My worldview pretty much changes from minute to minute these days!"

"As it should, my friend. As it should."

CHAPTER 39

*T*he pair continued to study the peculiar contraption, occasionally peering into the sky, and then to the hole in the mountain, then back to the time machine.

"One-Zero," Nicky Neill's voice was low but anxious, "what about that guy in the tunnel? What do we do when he comes back? He's from this place, you know?"

One-Zero shot his companion a wink. "I'm runnin' low on answers, pard. You'll have to do the thinkin' for a spell. You tell me what happens next."

"Oh, I get it. We wait for him to come out and then we follow him. Where he leads us is likely where we'll find my dad."

"How do you know that?" One-Zero maintained his scrutiny of the doorway.

"Because this is where the trail leads. And I'm pretty sure there's no other trail but this one."

"Hmm." One-Zero placed a hand on the boy's shoulder. "Well, there you go."

Nicky Neill stepped away from the device and crept back to the opening between the two great boulders. Dropping to his knees, he peered through the fissure and studied the dark cavity in the mountainside. He understood it to be a portal now, a gateway between two worlds. The hole in the rock remained agape. He wedged himself into a comfortable position, prepared to wait out the reappearance of the Mayan with the smoldering eyes. His vigil was short lived.

"One-Zero! He's here!" Nicky Neill stifled the urge to shout.

"Game on, huh?" One-Zero crowded in beside his accomplice. "Now the real fun starts!"

Framed in the opening, the man with burning eyes straddled the present and the past. For an instant, he faced the
intruders, hands on hips, while he cast his terrible gaze across
the landscape. Then he spun about and addressed someone in
the tunnel. His barrage of verbal abuse easily carried to the
mass of boulders. Nicky Neill spied Xac-Mal kneeling in the
doorway. The old priest was on the receiving end of the
assault. He took his licks like a schoolboy cornered in the prin-
cipal's office.

Moments later, Xac-Mal came to his feet and shuffled
backward into the tunnel, never once raising his head. Jaguar
Man stepped back as well. His arms left his side and shot skyward. A booming refrain issued from his mouth. Nicky Neill
recognized the words. Then a terrible noise shattered the air.
The enormous slab of stone began to grind back into its niche.
Slowly, forcefully, the door shut itself.

Jaguar Man remained in place, facing the expanse of stone.
When he was satisfied, he turned away from the portal and
stared long and hard into the distance. Although Nicky Neill
and One-Zero were well hidden from the man's view, the boy
was afraid that this individual could see through stone in
order to expose anyone who did not belong in his world.

Seconds ticked by and Jaguar Man made no movement in
their direction. His bearing gave no indication that he was
aware of their presence. Finally, he pushed back his cape and
set off at a brisk pace in the direction of a dense wall of jungle.

"One-Zero," Nicky Neill sighed, "I don't trust this guy at
all. Do you think it's safe to follow him?"

"Oh, sure. 'Bout as safe as stealing salmon from a grizzly!
But we don't have a whole lot of choice. We'll keep our distance and do our best not to give ourselves away."

Nicky Neill scrambled through the opening and skirted
the rock pile. One-Zero was fast on his tail. They made a beeline for the jungle's edge and eased into the brush. From there,
they spied a narrow trail. It wasn't long before they caught

sight of a jaguar robe and a dazzling feather headdress bobbing against the emerald backdrop of the forest.

Jaguar Man was not one to tarry. His walking pace was similar to One-Zero's, which meant Nicky Neill was forced to jog to keep the man in sight. Every fifteen or twenty yards, the pursuers arrested their progress and melted into the vegetation in the event their guide became suspicious.

Nicky Neill and One-Zero followed their prey for a half hour, keeping to the well-worn path. At a particular bend in the trail, however, their plan evaporated.

"One-Zero, did my eyes just quit or is that guy really gone?" Nicky Neill reined in his pursuit and backed into the foliage at trail's edge.

"He's gone, all right. But where he's gone may not be a place we ought to rush into." He surveyed the trail momentarily. "Pick a side, I'll take the other."

"What are you getting at?"

"He's gone off trail. This path is a diversion now. We're looking for another route, the one our guide's on."

"Gotcha." Nicky Neill hesitated. "Uh, traipsing through the bush is risky, don't you think?"

"Yeah, that's true. So take it slow and easy. You know what I mean?"

"I do." Nicky Neill stepped off the footpath and moved deeper into the undergrowth. Images of black spines and vipers, and booby traps, measured his progress.

At one point a swath of odd, purplish plants appeared in front of him. Beyond the plants a dense wall of bamboo jutted forward at an unnatural angle. Alarms sounded in Nicky Neill's ears, but he pressed ahead and poked a toe into the mass. With nervous anticipation he shifted his weight onto his lead foot. As he did, his heel sailed out from under him and it was all he could do to keep himself from falling.

"Whoa! What the—?" Nicky Neill lowered himself to his knees and parted the mat of vegetation with a quivering hand. The opening he created became a window for a spectacular view. "One-Zero!" he hissed. "This way. You have to see this!" In short order, his friend was crouching beside him, peering through the break in the flora.

"Well, what do you know? You found the lost world, Nick. Ain't it somethin'?"

CHAPTER 40

*T*he pair's point of observation was the lip of a sheer cliff, part of a towering rock wall that ran from one side of a lush river valley to the other. From where they crouched, the drop to the valley floor appeared to be several hundred feet. Off to their right a breathtaking waterfall exploded from the vegetation and cascaded into vapor-thick air, plummeting into a glistening, fast-moving river. The river itself disappeared into the base of the wall.

Nicky Neill directed his gaze from the hypnotic meeting of the waters to the green countryside upriver. In that instant, his breath was stolen. Again. At first glance, his brain screamed *mirage*. He blinked, and blinked a second time. It was no illusion.

A vision of majestic accomplishment towered over the fertile plain on the river's far bank. What he saw was a city unlike any his imagination could have conjured. Massive towers of square-cut stone rose high into the morning sun, and beyond them brilliant red pyramids climbed even higher. The peaks of every structure were adorned with brightly colored temples or palaces. Banners and streamers fluttered from every eave. In the shadows of the magnificent skyscrapers, a continuous sprawl of lesser structures filled the spaces below. Where the stone architecture ended, a dense dispersal of humble, thatch-roofed dwellings stretched at least a half mile to the ribbon of emerald forest that bordered the river's edge. Thin columns of gray smoke rose toward the cloud-choked sky. Everywhere he looked he saw people, scurrying like ants on a picnic blanket.

He redirected his attention to the urban zone. Everything in the hub of the city was connected to everything else by stone bridges or exquisite arches. Zipper-like stairways zigzagged throughout the inner core, rising and falling in every direction.

"Good golly, One-Zero," Nicky Neill murmured. "What have we stumbled into?"

"A time capsule. And a well-preserved one at that. What say we take a closer look?"

"You mean, go down there, in broad daylight?"

"No, not yet anyway. I was referrin' to a bird's-eye view." One-Zero rolled onto his side and dragged up his pouch. Peeling back the cover flap, he inserted his hand and withdrew a shiny black cylinder. "This is a memento of my life at sea." Catching the ends of the cylinder with both hands, he pulled it apart and passed the extended version to the boy.

"A telescope!" Nicky Neill assumed a prone position and rested the telescope on the back of his left hand. Once the device was sighted, he set about scoping the panorama below. After several minutes had passed, One-Zero intervened.

"Okay, pard, paint me a picture. Lay out the details."

"It's unbelievable, man! No lie!" Nicky Neill twisted his head away from the eyepiece. "Do you want to see for yourself?"

"No, brother, I want you to describe it to me."

"Okay, here goes." Nicky Neill returned his eye to the spyglass and exhaled. "There's a high wall that runs the length of the city. All along the base of it are stalls, one after another. It's a marketplace! I recognize ears of corn and piles of tomatoes...and huge clusters of peppers. My gosh, they're selling so much stuff, I can't make it all out. Oh, wait! I see iguanas hanging by their tails...and snakes, too! And carcasses of deer, I think, and goats and pigs! And lots of turkeys and chickens. There's people selling blankets and clothing, pottery, furniture...and hammocks, beautiful hammocks. You know, it looks a whole lot like the market in Palenque."

"Yeah," One-Zero smiled, "some things are slow to change. What else do you see?"

"Well...it's the people. They're all ages. And everyone is in motion. But they're not like the Lacandon, not exactly. They look, uh, prosperous, I guess. I mean, most of them are wearing colorful clothes, and lots of them have on jewelry. And everyone is wearing sandals! No one is barefoot. Oh, man! One-Zero, I notice something else, too. A lot of these people are pudgy, fat even! I don't recall seeing any fat Lacandon, do you?"

"Good point, Nick. Now that you mention it, no, I don't. What else do you make out down there?"

"Um, let me see." Nicky Neill tilted the telescope away from the market and began to sweep his gaze in slow, broad strokes. Then his body went rigid. "Oh, my gosh! It's him! It's Jaguar Man! He's coming down a trail, moving towards the city. Here, see for yourself." Nicky Neill passed the spyglass to his companion.

"Hmm, that's him, all right. The trail must have dropped at the waterfall; that's why he seemed to disappear." One-Zero sat upright and extended the telescope to Nicky Neill. "Keep an eye on him for as long as you can. Find out where he's headed. I'm gonna take a closer look at the trail. Whatever you do, don't leave this spot."

"Right, I'll sit tight and try to keep an eye on our guy." Nicky Neill swung the telescope up to his eye. "Hey!" he called out. "Don't do anything too exciting without me!"

"Right, pard." One-Zero laughed. "I'll keep that in mind."

Nicky Neill trained his scope on the keeper of the mountain door and followed him into the city. He was more than happy to keep tabs on Jaguar Man from a distance. Up close, the guy was too fearsome for comfort.

CHAPTER 41

*J*aguar Man changed his course just before he reached the outer limits of the marketplace. Rather than enter the bustling commercial zone, he veered onto a narrow side trail that angled uphill, away from the city center. Nicky Neill lost sight of him when he passed into a dense cluster of banana trees.

"Cripes! I lost him!" A wave of panic swept over the boy. "Hah! There you are, chief!" Jaguar Man resurfaced along a walkway atop the perimeter wall. He climbed a nearby staircase to a second level and proceeded smartly along a broad thoroughfare. It was then that Nicky Neill noticed how passersby scurried to get out of his way. Even his own people were afraid of him.

For the next several minutes, Nicky Neill worked to keep Jaguar Man in his sights. What complicated his task was the intricate nature of the city's architecture. Each time he thought he'd lost his man, the flowing jaguar cape would resurface on a level above the previous sighting. It occurred to Nicky Neill that his quarry had a specific destination in mind. He was moving toward the most massive pyramid.

Nicky Neill raised the spyglass in order to study Jaguar Man's obvious destination. The structure was a mindbender. It was so massive that Nicky Neill concluded it was an actual mountain, that the Mayans had carved out their pyramid rather than constructed it. At its base a broad courtyard stood empty. It wasn't long before Jaguar Man appeared on the scene.

As soon as the doorkeeper set foot on the courtyard, a party of soldiers burst from the shadows and formed a line in front of him. Each warrior bristled with armaments—clubs, axes, long spears, and curious devices draped across their shoulders. They wore armor, too, covering every part of their bodies.

One of the soldiers stepped forward to confer with the important visitor. They spoke, briefly, before the two of them strode across the courtyard and disappeared in the shadows. After a moment, the leader of the soldiers reappeared and signaled to his troops. Two of the men broke rank and marched toward the tall steps of the pyramid at the courtyard's edge. The two warriors skillfully mounted the giant stairs, but some fifteen or twenty steps up, they stopped. One of them knelt low and appeared to polish the stone in front of him.

Nicky Neill abandoned the pair of soldiers and began searching for Jaguar Man. He was nowhere in sight. At that moment, the boy realized he had lost him. He rescanned the surface of the courtyard. As he did, he noticed that all the soldiers in formation were craning their necks upward in the direction of their comrades on the steps. Nicky Neill followed their gaze. He was shocked to discover that an opening had appeared in the steps themselves. The two soldiers had taken up positions on either side of the portal. Their weapons were at the ready.

"What the heck?" Nicky Neill murmured to himself. "What's going on up there?" He adjusted his grip on the spyglass and held his breath for a steadier picture.

Something began to emerge from the hole in the stairs. It appeared slowly, in fits. It occurred to Nicky Neill that an animal of some sort was being led from its cage. The doorkeeper was going to perform a ritual. But as he observed the scene, the creature moved from the opening into the daylight. It was two-legged, perhaps a bear. The animal slowly rose up to its full height and rubbed its eyes, struggling to cope with the blinding effect of an intense sun.

The creature stretched and angled its head from one side to the other, working the cricks out of its neck. Something inside Nicky Neill began to quiver. He realized he was watching a man, not an animal. And something about the man was familiar to him.

In spite of his trembling hands, Nicky Neill looked the individual over from head to toe and back again. With each passing second a flood of insufferable emotions swelled inside of him.

Unlike the Mayan warriors at his side, the man wore a shirt and trousers. A thick growth of beard covered his face. The man yawned. A rain of tears burst from Nicky Neill's eyes and obscured his vision. It did not matter. He had seen enough.

The man on the steps, the filthy, disheveled individual struggling with the glaring sunlight, was his dad. Dr. Carpenter was alive.

CHAPTER 42

A scream welled in Nicky Neill's throat. But it lodged in his larynx and shattered in his mouth. All that emerged was a ruptured squawk.

"One-awwk!" Laughing and crying simultaneously, the boy cleared his throat and made a second effort. "One-Zero! One-Zero!" He dropped the telescope and jumped to his feet. "It's him! It's him! It's Dad! He's alive!" His celebratory jig ended when he tripped over his own feet and crashed face first into a clump of prickly flowers. Rolling aside, he scurried on his knees to the observation point and snatched up the spyglass again.

The scene had not changed. Dr. Carpenter remained on the steps above the courtyard, hemmed in by the two soldiers

"At long last a view of Dr. Carpenter; captive yet alive"

who had fetched him. They appeared to be waiting for something. While they stood there, Nicky Neill looked his father over as closely as he could. He did not appear to be injured, nor did he cower in the presence of his guards. His hair was wild, and Nicky Neill had never seen him with a beard before. In spite of the circumstances, he didn't seem too worse for wear.

"What the cow dung is he doing there?" he murmured. "Are you living there, Dad? Do they keep you locked up in the heart of that danged pyramid? Hang on, Dad! Hang on! We're coming to get you." Then a familiar voice sounded over his shoulder.

"When did you take up talkin' to yourself, pard?"

"One-Zero! Oh, my gosh, I'm glad to see you! I found my dad! He's down there, right now! Jaguar Man and a bunch of warriors, they've got him. We've got to get him out. Now, right now!"

"Whoa, son. Scale back a notch. Tell me what you know." One-Zero knelt beside his companion. Nicky Neill passed the telescope to his friend and while he focused on the scene he told him about everything he had observed. One-Zero nodded occasionally as Nicky Neill spoke.

"Ahh," he said, after several minutes had passed. "So..."

"What is it? What's happening?" Nicky Neill crowded closer.

"Jaguar Man just appeared. And he's not alone. He's got a couple of other priests in tow." One-Zero hesitated, then continued. "Hmm, they're climbing up to your dad...now they're tying his hands behind his back. Here, you take the scope again. Keep me informed."

"Oh, man! Now they're all moving higher up towards the top!"

Jaguar Man was in the lead, flanked by two other priests. Behind them trailed Dr. Carpenter and his warrior escorts. Bringing up the rear, a contingent of soldiers tagged along in tight formation.

The climb to the summit of the pyramid was steep and long, but the group forged ahead, never once pausing to rest or look back. When they reached the crest the priests disappeared into a shrine, leaving their prisoner surrounded by a phalanx of soldiers.

"The priests ducked into the temple, One-Zero. What are they up to?"

"They're probably tending to a ritual or some such. Supplicating the gods, lighting incense, that sort of thing."

"Oh." Nicky Neill blinked in the eyepiece. "So, why did they take Dad up there?"

One-Zero exhaled slowly, squinting into the sun. "I'm not sure yet," he said at last, speaking as if his mind was occupied on some faraway place. "But I don't like it."

More time passed before all three priests reappeared. They had changed clothes while they were gone. Now they sparkled brilliantly as they filed out of the structure, led by Jaguar Man. At his direction, the soldiers who held the prisoner stepped toward the entrance to the shrine. All the others fell in behind them. Two men emerged from the building dressed in long, white, simple tunics. Each of them clutched an object in his hand.

In synchronized fashion, the entire party moved out from the shadows cast by the temple. The men in white walked to opposite corners of the platform. Then, a blast of trumpets echoed across the valley.

"What the heck?" Nicky Neill looked to One-Zero. "What's that racket about?"

"Seems they want the city's attention. Look the place over. See how the people respond."

Nicky Neill returned to the eyepiece and began a slow sweep of the landscape. One-Zero was right. People were putting a halt to whatever they were doing. Soon a mass movement was underway as citizens began filing toward the central plaza. As the crowd gathered, the trumpets continued to blare.

Meanwhile, Dr. Carpenter remained wedged between the two soldiers, a reluctant observer to a gathering of the city's inhabitants that increasingly bore the earmarks of something ominous.

Nicky Neill longed for telepathic powers, some way, any way to send a signal to his dad. But he was powerless. There was nothing for him to do except watch. And wait.

CHAPTER 43

When the central plaza became packed with people, and the remainder of the population was streaming in that direction, the trumpets fell silent.

The center of the city was perfectly aligned with the great pyramid. By looking upward, every citizen had a clear view of the summit as well as the soldiers and priests and the bedraggled prisoner in their custody.

The two soldiers on either side of Dr. Carpenter seized him by the arms and marched him toward the edge of the platform. For an instant it appeared they intended to hurl him over the edge.

"One-Zero! They're going to..."

"Easy, son. It's not time for that yet."

"Yet? Did you say 'yet'?"

"Watch. And pay attention to every detail, hear? We're gonna have to know our way around the city, and that big pyramid in particular."

Nicky Neill returned the telescope to his eye. He would do as his friend suggested.

The soldiers escorted their prisoner to the precipice and held him in place for all to see. Jaguar Man moved in beside them. His arms shot skyward and the entire population in the plaza below imitated his gesture.

"He's stirrin' 'em up," One-Zero said.

"Why? And why have my dad on hand for this? I don't get it."

"It's just a hunch that our friend is blamin' your father for the excitement in the cave this morning. And I reckon he's also writing off any other problems these folks are having, all on account of the professor bein' here."

Nicky Neill lowered the telescope. "So, you're telling me that Jaguar Man is blaming my dad for anything that might be going wrong in this valley?"

"Pretty much. It's an old trick that elites have employed for a long time. It's called scapegoating, and it usually pays off."

"I don't like where this is going, One-Zero. Not at all." Nicky Neill spun around to face his friend. "We came here to save Dad, not punish him."

One-Zero locked eyes with his companion. "Your daddy is in a pickle, that's a fact. If it weren't for him, we'd never have upset the Lacandon. Likewise, we wouldn't have caused the excitement in the cave. When your father came down here, he assumed there'd be risks. He was prepared to accept them. Every action has its consequences, don't ya know?"

"But...you make it all sound so matter-of-fact. Dang, what can we do about this?"

The gleam returned to One-Zero's eyes. "Well, we'll take some action ourselves, Nick. An' you can bet we'll have a few consequences of our own in mind."

A colossal clap of thunder exploded overhead and a torrent of rain burst from the patchwork of wispy ashen clouds. Nicky Neill began to laugh out loud and One-Zero followed suit.

"This rain is not even coming from those clouds, is it?" Nicky Neill gasped, turning his face skyward.

"Nope, it ain't. It's all part of the magic of this lost world! And look yonder." One-Zero gestured toward the city.

People were fleeing the plaza as the monsoon intensified. Strings of quivering lightning exploded from thin air and licked at the rooftops along the city's skyline. Even the soldiers on the great pyramid cowed in the face of the storm. In short order, the priests hastened into the temple, while the military escort led the prisoner back to his holding place. Nicky Neill watched them as they scurried down the steps. He counted up from the base of the structure and committed the number of steps to memory. He observed as his father stepped into a hole in the stairs and disappeared from view. When he lowered the spyglass and turned to relay what he had seen to his friend, he found One-Zero sprawled on his back, mouth open, a wild-eyed grin plastered across his face.

CHAPTER 44

*T*he two infiltrators remained stretched out in the downpour long enough for puddles to form at their sides. The unexpected rain had burst from the sunny, cloud-pocked sky like a godsend. Between fits of euphoria and damped-down anxiety, Nicky Neill struggled to make sense of reality. At some point, he began to laugh. Soon he was engulfed in laughter until breathing became a challenge. As he gasped for air, he became aware of One-Zero laughing beside him. In that moment, he understood why his friend wore a constant grin on his face.

One-Zero eventually sat upright and suggested they seek cover and indulge in Hector's provisions. The pair sloshed to their feet and splashed back into the glistening jungle behind them in search of a sheltering location.

"There," One-Zero pointed. "There's our tipi."

Twenty yards into the forest, a towering tree rose into the canopy. Parasitic vines had long squeezed their host and had effectively strangled the great giant. Now the vines were the tree and what had once been a proud hardwood was a hollowed-out skeleton of itself. And that hollow was immense, sheltering, and dry.

Nicky Neill and One-Zero checked their refuge for vipers and cleared the cobwebs before moving in.

"Oh, man!" Nicky Neill sighed, easing himself into position. "First a shower, now a steam bath!"

"Yeah, jungle livin', huh?" Upon settling in, One-Zero drew up Hector's bag and began fishing through the contents. "So, compadre, what'll it be? Dried meat and oranges, or oranges and dried meat?"

"Thanks for the offer, One-Zero, but if it's all the same to you, I'll have the peanut butter and honey sandwich and the rest of the Oreos!"

"Just like I figured, you want the dried meat and oranges!"

They ate in silence. In the shelter of the hollowed-out tree, all of Nicky Neill's questions had been replaced by a tremendous sensation of relief. After so many weeks, after so much struggle and hardship, they had found his dad. And he was alive. Before long, he began to think about Ploox. He wished his friend were with him now, experiencing this lost world. Up until this leg of the journey, they had done everything together. It didn't seem right without him. But then, his buddy was now a king! He had duties, responsibilities. Nicky Neill felt himself choking up. Ploox, he smiled proudly, had to make sure the sun rose and set like it should.

Although the rainwater had evaporated off his face, Nicky Neill became conscious of something else streaming down his cheeks. With a clumsy swipe, he blotted at a rivulet of tears. Images of the gang back home flooded his imagination. If only those guys could see Ploox now. The kid they loved to tease was no longer that kid. They did not know Ploox the adventurer, the hero, the lover, and now, the king! Nicky Neill shook his head and sighed. Of all the friends he'd ever had, Ploox was by far the best and the truest. He was proud of the changes Ploox had undergone in his life and the truths he had discovered about himself.

Nicky Neill stopped dabbing at the tears. He loved his friend like a brother. His dad was alive. Life was grand.

CHAPTER 45

*T*he next thing Nicky Neill remembered was One-Zero tugging at his pant leg.

"Huh?" He sprang upright. "What is it? What's happening?"

"Easy, pard, you been nappin'. Mother Nature gave you a break."

"Hmm. Wow! How long have I been sleeping?" A sense of urgency jolted Nicky Neill's entire body.

"Take it easy, little brother. You've been out for a few hours. But you haven't missed anything. In fact, the rain is just now taperin' off."

"A few hours? That can't be! Oh, gosh, One-Zero! What are we doing? What's our plan? Where's Dad?"

"Listen up," One-Zero said, in his normal, matter-of-fact tone. "It'll be dark before long and time for us to make our move. Are you up to it?"

"Come on, One-Zero! Does a monkey pee in a tree? You know I'm ready. What's our plan?"

"Good. Just checkin'. As for a plan, well, there really ain't one. We just gotta do what's gotta be done. Plain and simple."

"And?" Nicky Neill grinned back at him. "Describe plain and simple."

"Well, from here we follow Jaguar Man's trail down to the city. Somewhere along the way we bear down on a clothesline and suit up Maya style. Then we make a beeline for that mountain of a pyramid. From there, we spring your pap and slip out of town. On the way home we grab Ploox, hook up with Jorge, and get back in time for supper with Helen. Complicated, huh?"

"You know, One-Zero, you've got a real way with words. And all this time I figured that bringing Dad home would be a challenge."

As darkness began to settle upon the jungle, One-Zero led the way out of the forest and on to Jaguar Man's trail. Traveling the worn path was easy until they reached the waterfall. The stone steps that followed the water down were moss-covered and slippery from the constant blanket of mist that bathed the surrounding jungle. When they reached the bottom, their surroundings were murky at best.

"It was all so clear from the cliff," Nicky Neill said. "But down here it's a different story...like shadows on top of shadows. Can you see anything?"

"Naw." One-Zero moved alongside his partner. "You're right about the visibility; it's pea soup, all right. But I ain't seein' with my eyes at the moment."

"Well, if you're not using your eyes, what then? Did you pull some special goggles out of that magic pouch of yours?"

"Listen up, Nick. Use your mind like a camera. It works like a charm, no batteries necessary."

"Okay," Nicky Neill squinted into the gathering pitch, "what are you talking about?"

"Close your eyes. Now, envision the pictures you observed from up there on the bluff. You spent a lot of time eyeballin' the city and everything around it. You also scoped out the river, especially where the waterfall emptied into it. Think about it."

Nicky Neill closed his eyes. With a little coaxing, his mind's eye opened and when it did, images of the city, the marketplace, the pyramid, and most of all, his dad flooded into a parade of pictures that began to loop through his brain.

"Go down to the river and locate Jaguar Man crossing it. Do you see him?" One-Zero paused briefly. "Now, follow him through the forest, all the way into the city...memorize his route. When you open your eyes, all of your pictures will remain available to you. Do you understand?"

Nicky Neill nodded.

"All right, let's start at the top. Retrace your steps to the stairway. Climb down, just like before. When you reach the bottom, open your eyes." One-Zero waited patiently.

Nicky Neill's eyes popped open. "Oh, my gosh, it's totally dark now!"

"That it is. You ready to lead the way?"

"Yeah," Nicky Neill sighed, easing back into the world outside his mind. "I'm ready."

They moved across the river, using the same chain of boulders as Jaguar Man. On the far side, the path revealed itself as a dark stain threading through a murky cloud of forest and shadows. A cool breeze rattled the leaves above their heads, sending a cascade of water down upon them.

"Brrr!" Nicky Neill shivered. "And I was mostly dry except for my feet."

"Right." One-Zero chuckled. "They don't call it a rain forest for nothin'."

The pair continued their trek at a snail's pace. A half hour into their hike, they spotted the glow of multiple cooking fires in the near distance.

"People ahead," Nicky Neill whispered, stopping to crouch low and scout the landscape. "We're at the edge of the farms that ring the city. Beyond the farms is a string of villages, and then a continuous belt of community. After that is the marketplace. It butts up against the wall that surrounds the city." Nicky Neill twisted around to look into One-Zero's face. "We're there, man. Roll out your plan."

"Let's check for laundry," One-Zero whispered.

"You lead," Nicky Neill whispered back.

They became shadow-like, sticking close to the wall of jungle, then crawling low to the earth when the tree line dissipated. Their goal was to reach the first cluster of dwellings undetected, where, hopefully, they would encounter laundry. But there was none to be found.

"I don't recall all these people walking around naked, One-Zero. What gives?"

One-Zero responded with the slap of his forehead. "Doggone, Nick! We're barkin' up the wrong tree. If you lived here, where would you scrub your threads?"

"Ah, dang! The river, of course!"

"Right." One-Zero's grin practically glowed in the dark. "Let's go!"

They backtracked several hundred yards, then cut across the trail and made a beeline for the river. From there, they followed the waterway upstream where they found themselves neck deep in laundry. Clothing was draped over and around every available rock, bush, and tree limb.

Within the first few minutes of sorting, Nicky Neill located a plain, almost dry, tunic. It easily slipped over his jeans and T-shirt. "Voila!" he exclaimed. "Behold, Nick the Mayan!"

"Good for you, peasant boy." One-Zero laughed. "Maybe you can help me locate the jumbo department?" After a string of disappointments, he settled upon a blanket. Nicky Neill watched as his friend cut a long gash in the center of the cover and proceeded to pull it over his head.

"There! I feel more like an Inca than a Maya, but it'll do. Let's get on with it."

This time One-Zero took the lead. It wasn't long before they came upon another cluster of huts. At one edge of the knot of dwellings, a small fire glowed faintly. The two trespassers paused to check each other's appearance.

"Better roll those pant legs up, Nick."

"Right, thanks. Oh, gosh, what about the boots? They stick out like two sore thumbs!" Nicky Neill kicked his boots off, along with his soppy socks, and stashed them in a clump of brush.

One-Zero shook his head in feigned disbelief. His blanket flapped loosely at his knees, revealing at least a third of his non-Mayan body. He shot his companion a cat-in-the-cream look before he slipped his pants off and tied them around his waist. Then he buried his sandals in the brush alongside Nicky Neill's boots.

"You don't have to go barefoot, too," Nicky Neill whispered.

"Hey, if we have to walk through fire, I can't let you have all the fun."

"What fire?"

One-Zero did not answer. He had already skirted the dim shadows cast by the fire pit and was off, moving down a narrow trail through the forest in the direction of the city proper.

CHAPTER 46

$\mathcal{N}$icky Neill quickly caught up with One-Zero. He was glad his friend had taken the lead again. Now that they were moving into a more populated zone, experience in such places could make all the difference.

In the course of their trek to reach the city's outer wall, the pair passed through multiple villages and dozens of isolated huts. Oddly, they encountered very few people. At one point, they skirted a simple hut where a small fire still glowed in the open entryway. A family of five nestled snugly in a large hammock. It was another image Nicky Neill would never forget. Without electricity to propel them, people bedded down when night settled in. He continued to reflect about that observation as they maneuvered through the shadows.

"Hold up!" One-Zero signaled a halt. "Let's scout this." Both men dropped to a knee and launched a careful survey of the area before them.

In the near distance, the towering outer wall of the city loomed in front of them, rising into the night sky like a monstrous ocean wave.

"There." One-Zero pointed to the right. "There's a door. And it's open."

"Whatever you say, boss! Are there any guards around?"

"Naw, none that I can make out. Here goes."

One-Zero rose to a crouch and set off toward the wall. Nicky Neill was close behind him.

When they reached the wall, One-Zero pulled Nicky Neill close. "We go in together, pard." They passed as one through the break, into a world that chose to forget time.

It was tomb-like inside. Intuitively, they kept to the wall, moving uphill as they went. After twenty yards they reached a stairway. They began their ascent as their eyes struggled to adjust to the darkness. Upon climbing a dozen tall steps, they smacked into another wall. Nicky Neill's hands shot up and his fingers glided over the cool surface until it led him to another staircase. This one rose upward at a steep angle to their left. By the time they reached the top, Nicky Neill's thighs were burning and his breathing was painfully labored.

"Yay!" he gasped in relief. "It's about time."

"I agree," One-Zero huffed. "I think we've arrived."

The pair lingered on the expanse of stone at the stairway's landing, struggling to catch their wind. The cityscape that confronted them, however, stole their breath yet a second time.

"Is this real?" Nicky Neill gawked. "I've seen some things on this trip, One-Zero, but this...this is in a class of its own."

"Whew," One-Zero sighed. "It definitely ain't somethin' you see every day."

The city surrounded them, stretching into a continuous mass of streets, structures, fountains, and courtyards aglow from the lights of a thousand tiny lanterns. Narrow streets and alleyways trailed off in obscure directions, and small mountains rose and fell across the entire horizon. Nicky Neill recognized the mountainous profiles; they were pyramids. There were many gods in Mayan cosmology and here, in this incredible city, Nicky Neill could see that each of them had a home. There was more; the place emitted a spectacular iridescence, mostly reddish in hue, but all the other colors of a rainbow as well quivered across the cityscape. For a moment, Nicky Neill forgot to breathe.

"Set?" One-Zero tapped his companion's shoulder.

"Huh? Oh, yeah. I'm ready. Lead the way."

One-Zero stepped forward cautiously, engaging all of his senses in an effort to detect the presence of others.

"Wait!" Nicky Neill tugged at his friend's blanket. "Hear that?"

"Yes." One-Zero nodded. "I hear it. Voices, lots of 'em. Somethin' big must be going on this evening."

"Right," Nicky Neill whispered. "Must be why there's no one on the street. That's good for us."

"We'll find out soon enough. We're headed in the general direction of whatever commotion is underway."

Moving through the deserted city was unnerving but easy. Their firm path ran between, beneath, and around all manner of man-made structures.

One-Zero waved Nicky Neill over. They had reached a fork in their path. "Right or left? Your call."

"Right," Nicky Neill replied.

"Right it is."

Their new course led them around a circular tower that connected with a steep flight of narrow steps. At the top of their climb, they found themselves at the edge of a broad terrace. They hesitated, listening for human presence. When they detected none, they crossed the open expanse and entered a lush, manicured garden. But they soon left the greenbelt behind, striking out once again over the cool stone walkway.

A block or more beyond the garden, their path angled upward at a steep pitch. Before long both trespassers were huffing and puffing, with no end in sight. Somewhere, in the midst of their ascent, Nicky Neill detected a low rumbling noise. He stopped moving and cupped a hand to his ear.

"There's that crowd sound again! We're getting closer."

"Right," One-Zero panted between labored breaths. "It's the roar of the crowd, for sure."

"Come on, we've got to find out what's happening." After a few paces Nicky Neill stopped again and turned to his friend. "One-Zero, what if...what if my dad's involved in this...in some way?"

"We'll respond to what we find, son. That's our only recourse. Keep movin'."

In spite of the vigorous ascent, Nicky Neill quickened his stride. Moments later he was jogging. One-Zero was close on his heels. The effect of their rapid advance soon took its toll on Nicky Neill. Just as he sensed he was about to collapse, he breeched the incline. In that same instant, he threw himself to the ground. One-Zero belly-flopped beside him seconds later.

"Oh, my gosh!" Nicky Neill struggled to breathe and talk at the same time. "What have we gotten ourselves into?"

Some two or three hundred yards ahead of them, and stretching beyond that as far as they could see, came a wide column of people. Each person held a candle or lantern. In one voice they sang out a jubilant chant.

Nicky Neill stared in disbelief. The entire population of the city and most of the countryside was jammed together, pressed into a single, winding human serpent. And it was slithering directly toward their vantage point.

CHAPTER 47

"One-Zero! What's going on? We're trapped!"

"Beats me, but that's not the only crowd out for a stroll. Look yonder." He raised a finger and gestured over Nicky Neill's left shoulder.

"Oh, my gosh!" Nicky Neill gasped. "More of them!"

Approaching from another avenue, an equally animated swarm of Mayans marched in their direction. For an instant, a sour, sickly feeling flooded through Nicky Neill's gut. "We gotta move, One-Zero!" He sprang to his feet and darted up a tight alleyway behind them. One-Zero followed his lead. The narrow tunnel quickly emptied into a thoroughfare. Once again, they landed squarely in the path of an oncoming, chanting mob.

"What!" Nicky Neill exclaimed. He spun about to face One-Zero. "Back to the alley!" The pair backpedaled into the shadowy corridor and held their breath.

In a matter of seconds, tight gaggles of Mayans began filing past the alley's mouth, lurching and staggering and clinging to one another as if they couldn't make their way without their companions to lean upon. One of the trampers peeled away from his company and stumbled into the nearby side street. His forward progress was halted when his forehead collided with the wall. The man moaned, tilted backward, then steadied himself. He promptly hiked up his tunic and proceeded to urinate with wild abandon. Then he locked gazes with Nicky Neill. The two strangers were only inches apart. In a split second, Nicky Neill pitched his head between his legs and pretended to upchuck. The stranger laughed uproariously and swiveled to slap the boy's backside. In the process, he lost his grip on his tunic. He convulsed in stitches as his garment soaked up what was meant for the wall. His bladder emptied, the carefree soul shouted out a final piece of advice to Nicky Neill before plunging back into the river of citizens who continued to stream past.

"Some encounter, huh?" One-Zero stifled his urge to laugh out loud. "Quick thinkin', too!"

"That guy was stupid drunk! What's going on here? The whole city's gone crazy!"

"Only one thing I can imagine has this kind of effect on people." One-Zero grinned.

"Yeah? What's that? I'd like to know what makes an entire city lose its mind."

"Well, pard, I reckon this particular culprit is one you already know."

The intruders lingered in the alleyway until the last of the parade disappeared over a rise in the avenue.

"Okay, let's tag along." As if he perceived no personal risk, One-Zero stepped onto the empty pathway and set off in pursuit of the inebriated mass.

"What the—?" Nicky Neill hesitated, but only for an instant. "Hide in plain sight it is!" he muttered, sprinting to catch up to his friend. "You've got a lot of confidence in that blanket of yours."

They followed the mob at a safe distance until just like that, the whole rabble vanished.

"Hello?" One-Zero checked his progress. "That's a bit odd, ain't it?"

"First, the city makes them all loco," Nicky Neill marveled, "then it swallows them up...right in front of our eyes. What gives?"

A sly smile spread across One-Zero's face. "You notice how bright it is up ahead?"

"Yeah, now that you mention it. Must be a really big bonfire somewhere."

"Or a lot of small ones! Come on, let's have a look-see."

One-Zero turned away from the broad boulevard and slipped down a side street. Nicky Neill was close behind him.

Before long, the narrow lane intersected with another walkway that appeared to angle back in the direction where the sky was glowing. One-Zero veered down the new trail as if he knew where he was bound. He picked up the pace as well. The incandescence shimmering in the sky ahead grew more intense as the roar of thousands of voices split the air.

"Cripes!" Nicky Neill exclaimed. "We're right on top of them!"

"Not just yet!" One-Zero approached the corner of a nearby structure. "Time to move up in the world, my friend!" With a wink, he began to scale the building. Nicky Neill looked on as the blanket disappeared from sight. "Well?" a voice called down from the shadows. "You won't see squat from that alley!"

"Right! I'm coming up." Nicky Neill launched his ascent. Seconds later he reached the summit.

"Give me your hand, pard."

"Believe I will." One-Zero's viselike grip found his wrist and steadied him before hoisting him onto a gently sloping roof.

"I don't think anyone will pee on ya up here!" One-Zero's outline was illuminated by an eerie glow emanating from somewhere in the near distance. "Okay, then. Let's get closer and solve this riddle. Watch your step, Nick."

Two stories above the narrow alleyways, the pair advanced toward the light source. Two-dozen tentative paces delivered them to the roof's edge.

"Dang!" One-Zero muttered beneath his breath. "I climbed one buildin' too soon."

Nicky Neill eased in close behind his friend and peered over his shoulder. "How far do you think it is from our roof to that one?"

"Oh, in this dim light, I'd guesstimate between six and eight feet...ten at the most." He twisted his head to confront his companion. "We can climb down and scale back up on the other side. What do you say?"

Nicky Neill remained silent. After a moment, he offered his reply. "I'm barefoot. I jump better with my shoes off. I say we hop it!"

"Good call! Let's back up a bit. I don't know 'bout you, but I'm gonna need a run at this." With considerable care, they backpedaled a meaningful distance. "This oughta do it. See ya on the other side!" Without waiting for Nicky Neill's response, One-Zero bolted toward the precipice and launched himself for the opposite ledge. He jumped like a cat, a really big cat. "Okay, pard," he called back across the divide. "Your turn."

Nicky Neill hoisted his tunic and sucked down a lungful of night air. Then he sprinted for the ledge. His next conscious memory was of the landing and the impact against One-Zero's body. He stopped on a dime.

"Well done, little brother! Shall we continue?"

"Yeah, let's go." Nicky Neill readjusted his tunic and fell in behind his friend.

The pair executed two more leaps in their effort to draw as close to the light source as possible. When they reached the final structure, there was nowhere to go but up.

"We've arrived. If I've figured this right, whatever has got this city hoppin' will become apparent from this rooftop. Of course, on the other hand, we could just shinny off this building and find a good restaurant. I've got a powerful hankerin' for black beans and tortillas at this very moment."

"Sure, go ahead and make reservations for us while I take a peek at the other side." Without wasting any more time, Nicky Neill spun about and began to move up the gentle slope of the roof on all fours. Once he reached the peak, he wrapped his fingers around the crest and drew himself up until his head cleared the rooftop. At the same time, he became aware of his friend beside him.

"Okay," One-Zero sighed. "I'll eat later."

"Well," Nicky Neill extended his head over the crest, "we finally got a..." His words caught in his throat, as did the accompanying breath. He glanced, wild-eyed, at One-Zero. But his friend seemed unfazed. Nicky Neill, however, was wholly unprepared for what they saw.

CHAPTER 48

*T*he mystery behind the disappearance of the broad avenue that Nicky Neill and One-Zero had taken ended abruptly at the lip of an enormous depression. Similar streets angled in from different directions. Each of them terminated at the edge of the basin. A bolt of recognition pierced Nicky Neill's brain. The fragmented puzzle that had been growing throughout the evening began to take shape. He remained awestruck as hundreds of Mayans continued to flow off the streets and empty into what appeared to be an immense, smoking sinkhole.

"Welcome to fourteenth century Mesoamerica." An element of awe accented One-Zero's pronouncement.

The gates of Hell had been flung open, fires raged everywhere, and ordinary Mayans poured into the gaping pit, seemingly to be roasted alive. The smoke that wafted out of the great hole in the earth bore a rancid scent. Nicky Neill yearned to turn away, to avert his gaze and return to street level, but a fierce curiosity held him in place.

"What...what's happening here?" Nicky Neill's eyes remained riveted on the tumultuous event underway in the near distance. "I don't understand."

"There's no electrical service in this city, pard. In order to stage a nighttime show they have to rely on man's oldest friend. From the looks of it, it appears they've got it worked out. I count forty-five columns that surround the lower level. Those big dishes sproutin' out the top of each column are burning oil of some sort. And the long torches stickin' out of the walls are hewn from hardwood, likely dipped in the same oil. Yes, sir, Nick. These folks know what they're doin'."

"Of course! It's a stadium!"

"Now you've got it!" One-Zero shot him a wink. "When you asked me what could possibly have such a delirious effect on these people, you recall my response?"

"Yeah, you said it was likely something I already knew of. So?"

"So, look closely. If this is truly a stadium, what's about to happen here?"

"Oh, my gosh! There's going to be a game tonight! Everything we've seen, all the people, all the excitement...only sports drive people this bonkers!"

"What's comin' up here won't be just any old sporting event." One-Zero's gaze narrowed on his companion. "They're about to play the Ball Game, the oldest sport in this hemisphere."

"A ball game? Were balls even invented in the fourteenth century?"

"You'd have to know somethin' about the history of the rubber tree to appreciate this undertaking. Odds are, the Olmecs invented this game and the ball itself three thousand years before the Christian era began. In fact, the Aztecs referred to the Olmecs as the 'people who used rubber.' When the Europeans came on the scene, the Aztecs played this game on a grand scale. Huge crowds would be on hand, accompanied by heavy betting. I've read accounts of people losing food and clothing, not to mention jewelry and other artifacts of wealth. It's been recorded that people even wagered their children and their own freedom on the outcome."

"Are you kidding me? People did that sort of thing over a silly game?"

"This game," One-Zero weighed his words, "is part game and part ritual. It's complicated. Think about Ploox's role as king. A big part of his duty is to ensure the rising and setting of the sun. The world is an interconnected system and the Maya, and others throughout human history, have sought to keep the system stable. Instability leads to change, and change leads to unpredictability. At all cost, collapse is to be avoided."

He studied Nicky Neill's face. "The Ball Game is a game, for sure. But it's also symbolic of the workings of the world. As the Maya perceive it anyway."

"Hmm, I get it." Nicky Neill nodded in understanding. "But what makes them so...well...you know, like the guy in the alley?"

"That is the result of fermentation...corn or sugar cane, I suppose. Or any other handy commodity that grows 'round these parts that easily converts to alcohol!"

"Then, this Ball Game, it's a good thing, right? I mean, no sacrifices...just fun?"

One-Zero did not respond. Rather, his complete attention was focused on the extraordinary scene unfolding below.

Lively spectators flowed over the rim at street level and sank into the chasm like floodwaters seeking the lowest point of elevation. From the uppermost reaches of the stadium, a series of tall steps led downward. The levels of steps were concentric, encircling the entire space. At ground level, in the middle of the stadium, a great I-shaped courtyard constituted the playing field. Nicky Neill estimated the ball court's dimensions at roughly 300 feet in length by 100 feet in width. The walls at courtside sloped upward at an angle of approximately sixty degrees. This slope allowed for nearly twenty feet of additional playing surface. The oblique wall intersected with a vertical wall that climbed straight up at least another twenty or twenty-five feet. Cropping out from that towering embankment, evenly dispersed along the length of both sides of the court, were three imposing stone rings. The hole in the center of each ring appeared large enough to accommodate a human head. Any similarity to basketball was immediately stricken from Nicky Neill's mind as he pondered the massive rings. They were set into the wall, very near the top, in a vertical rather than a horizontal placement. Hurling something the size of a softball through one of those rings would constitute a near impossible task.

The top of the courtside wall comprised an observation deck that ran the length of both sides of the ball court. Beyond that, steep stairs rose all the way up to street level. Those steps served as seating for the raucous crowd that was rapidly packing the place.

"See that bottom row of stairs?" One-Zero spoke up at last. "That final row of seats is reserved for bigwigs. The folks who occupy the courtside level would be the top tier of elites, you know, priests and nobles, merchants and warriors and the like. An' that blockhouse at the end," he pointed out an ornate structure that Nicky Neill had assumed was a temple, "that's where the royals will view the action. I reckon that's the spot where our old friend, Jaguar Man, will show up next."

CHAPTER 49

"Okay," Nicky Neill asked, "what can you tell me about the Ball Game? I've been trying to work it out in my head but it's not happening."

"I've heard it called *pokatok*, also *pitz*. These days most folks just refer to it as the Ball Game. Two teams compete against each other. Gettin' the ball through those rings is an automatic game winner, but, as you can see," One-Zero nodded to the ball court, "that won't be an easy task."

"So," Nicky Neill interrupted, "do they throw the ball, or do they kick it?"

"Neither. They're not allowed to use their hands, an' the ball is too hard an' too heavy to kick."

"What! This is crazy!"

"You'll see directly how they move the ball. An' speakin' of that, you should know that the hunk of rubber about to fly around that court, it can weigh twenty pounds, or more. A ball to the head could kill a guy...a blow to the body will break ribs. It's not for the faint of heart."

"That's wild." Nicky Neill shuddered at the thought of cracking rib bones. "But it seems like the game could go on forever, trying to bounce the ball through one of those rings."

"No doubt. But makin' a ringer is not the only way to win. They have a point system. Gettin' the ball to strike one of those end walls," he gestured to the short walls in either end zone, "can rack up points. If the ball hits the playing surface, points are lost...if it bounces more than twice, more points are lost. Things like that. That's all I know."

A somber expression clouded Nicky Neill's face.

"Uh, is there any way this game could be connected to my dad?"

"I like the way your mind works, kid. But when you think like an adult, you're obligated to accept full-grown consequences."

"Why did I know you'd respond like that?" Nicky Neill looked deep into his friend's face.

"Because you're a truth-seeker now, son. If you pose the question, you expect a real answer."

"What are you saying, One-Zero?"

"I'm saying that oral history among the Mayans has it that one of the purposes of the Ball Game is to foretell the future."

"How does that relate to..." Nicky Neill's words trailed off into silence.

"These folks love a big event, like anyone else. A special occasion relieves boredom, punctuates the monotony of every-day life, and spices up the chores of daily living. Ya know what I mean?"

Nicky Neill nodded.

"And like I mentioned, there's gonna be gamblin' and high excitement. But on another level, Jaguar Man and the nobles who run this world, they may be lookin' for some answers. In particular, what to do about your dad. Somehow, the outcome of this game may provide them with an answer."

Nicky Neill stared hard into the depths of the ball court. "You could be totally wrong about this, right?"

"Absolutely," One-Zero acknowledged. "I'm not a fortune-teller...just a deductive thinker."

CHAPTER 50

*A*nimated Mayans continued to drain from the broad avenues into the great basin. Before long, the stadium was bursting with spectators. A legion of vendors plowed through the masses, hawking foodstuff.

"One-Zero, do you see those guys selling stuff, the ones with that big thing on their backs? What are they selling?"

One-Zero squinted into the distance. "Hah! Those fellas would be marketing joy juice! This crowd ain't reached its peak of rowdiness yet."

"But what is that thing on their backs? It looks like a burlap bag from here."

"That 'bag' is probably the lining of a tapir's stomach. I imagine they can tote three or four gallons in those bladders."

"Gross! How bad can that drink taste?"

"Well," One-Zero shrugged, "what I've sampled wasn't too bad!"

"Adults are weird." Nicky Neill studied the boisterous sea of ball fans. "I know these folks are letting off steam, but if there's one thing I've learned about grown-ups on this trip, it's that..." His words were interrupted by a thunderous blast that brought everything to a complete standstill.

"Here we go," One-Zero said.

A second series of blasts followed the first one. Nicky Neill recognized the powerful, piercing din of conch shells. No sooner had their echoes subsided than a chorus of flutes and whistles filled the air. From the corner of his eye, Nicky Neill caught sight of movement in the near end of the ball court. A colorful procession of eighteen individuals appeared around the corner of the great wall, moving toward a narrow staircase.

"Nobles, right?" Nicky Neill nodded at the pageant ascending the stairs. "I couldn't begin to describe these guys to anyone who's never seen them before."

"Recognize him?" One-Zero pointed to a straggler just rounding the edge of the wall.

"Oh, my gosh! It's him! It's Jaguar Man!"

"Indeed. Our man is the power behind the throne...no doubt about it."

When the lead entourage reached the top of the staircase, they moved into the open-sided blockhouse and took up seats that bordered the narrow walkway. When every noble—along with their wives and family—was seated, Jaguar Man climbed the stairs. At the summit, he bowed to the nobles and then proceeded to stride along the walkway to the middle of the stadium. There, he stopped and raised his arms to the calm, starry sky. An eerie silence hung over the entire scene. Had a cricket rubbed his wings together, it would have been audible to everyone in attendance. Jaguar Man turned to face the spectators on his side of the stadium. In a deep, booming voice he uttered a jagged stream of words. When he finished, he spun about on his heels and faced the opposite side of the basin. Once again, he barked out a message, the very same one he had previously delivered. When his voice fell silent, the crowd erupted.

Pandemonium returned, times two.

CHAPTER 51

*T*he jarring blare of conch shells ruptured the air again, accompanied by a grating chorus of flutes and whistles. Then a thunderous throbbing of drums entered the mix. When the music reached its peak, a knot of Indians exploded around the same section of wall that the nobles and Jaguar Man had appeared from only moments before. The screaming crowd came to its feet, and the level of noise soared to new heights as a second cluster of Indians raced onto the playing surface at the far end of the court.

"The teams are on the field," One-Zero announced. "Won't be long now."

Nicky Neill counted twenty-four players.

"One-Zero, mind if I check these guys out with your spyglass?"

"Good idea. Those fellas are not run-of-the-mill Mayans." He fished through his bottomless pouch and extended the instrument to his companion. "Take a lot of mental pictures, Nick. I doubt you'll see this sight again."

Nicky Neill turned the glass on the players in the near end of the court. He determined right away that they were not like other Mayans he had seen. These guys were angular and tightly muscled. Each one wore a wide, thick belt around his waist. On closer examination, he realized the belt was made from a single, horseshoe-shaped stone, secured by leather suspenders. Ankles and wrists sported similar protection. Knees and elbows were covered by what appeared to be ample leather wrap. Thick body armor covered their torsos, with a flap extending over their private parts.

"Good night!" Nicky Neill exclaimed. "How can these guys even move, let alone play?"

"We'll find out soon enough, won't we?" One-Zero shrugged.

All but two players wore tight-fitting leather helmets. The two athletes who did not bore elaborate headdresses instead. At first, Nicky Neill noticed a thick shock of colorful feathers sprouting above each man's head. But as they twisted and turned, he recognized the faces of animals looming over their foreheads. One mask was a representation of an eagle; the other was that of a jaguar. These two players were distinct in one additional manner; neither of them displayed the padded body armor of their teammates.

The players kept to their own ends of the ball court. For the next quarter hour, they stretched, tested and adjusted their equipment, and practiced their teamwork and game strategies. Several balls materialized and Nicky Neill found himself disappointed. He was anticipating something altogether exotic, a ball that would prove to be dangerous and challenging. What he observed appeared to be a mush ball of sorts, a leather sphere packed with rags or leaves or some other soft filler.

"What's so special about that ball, One-Zero? It's got no bounce, no life! If there's any rubber to it, it must be liquid."

"Hah!" One-Zero slapped his friend on the shoulder. "You usually don't rehearse the war with live ammunition."

Nicky Neill mulled his friend's comment over while he continued to watch the competitors in their warm-up.

"Game time!" One-Zero nudged his companion.

Nicky Neill swiveled the telescope away from the players, settling on a line of dignitaries filing out of the blockhouse. A stunningly regal individual strutted pompously at the head of a row of nobles, priests, and at the end, Jaguar Man. As the cast of luminaries strode toward mid-court, the mass of spectators came to their feet, cheering with renewed intensity.

When the leadership file reached the center of the stadium, they snapped to a halt and turned to face the two teams. The athletes had assembled at mid-court, facing each other across an imaginary line. They stood straight, proud, and clearly fearless of their opposition.

Following a single blast from a conch shell, the king raised his arms over his head and waited until the crowd's clamor subsided. Then he spoke. His voice was brittle and high-pitched, but he possessed the power of projection. He seemed to be addressing the ball players only.

When he was done, he stepped back. Jaguar Man promptly took the king's place. He lectured the two teams as well. Unlike the king, his voice was deep and his words resonated like cannon fire. When his speech ended he waved to one of the priests at the back of the line. This individual, looking like a quetzal bird personified, approached Jaguar Man and extended a pillow to him.

Nicky Neill trained his spyglass on the pillow and made out an object nestled in the cushion.

Jaguar Man reached out and grasped the object with both hands. He promptly raised it over his head. The crowd came to life with a vengeance.

Jaguar Man transferred the object to his right hand. It was a ball. As far as Nicky Neill could tell, it was at least the size of a cantaloupe, if not bigger. While Jaguar Man held the ball aloft, the players on the field scurried about. Four men from each team raced into the end zones, four positioned them-selves at mid-court, and four, including the two wearing ani-mal headdresses, aligned themselves in strategic patterns at center court.

"One-Zero, are we going to watch this entire game?"

"Naw, we can't afford to, seein' as how most of the city is in that coliseum. But, when a window opens that's been shut for five hundred years, men of knowledge have got to peer through it for a spell...wouldn't you agree?"

"Men of knowledge?" Nicky Neill scratched his head. "You sure have a way with words, One-Zero. And, yeah, I agree."

CHAPTER 52

$\mathcal{F}$or a moment Jaguar Man continued to keep the ball above his head, as far as his arm could extend. Then he performed a spectacular feat. His left arm rose up and made a broad sweep from one end zone to the other before shooting straight into the air as his right arm raced down and arched up again. On its way back up, he released the ball.

The ball completed an impressive arc and came down in the center of the court. Upon impact it exploded upward at a slanted angle as if it had a kinetic life of its own. One of the center-court players made a fantastic leftward leap and connected with it squarely on his stone girdle. Like a shot, the ball ricocheted forward, striking an opposing player in the chest. The man went down hard, landing on his back. A cloud of dust signaled his impact, but it did not obscure one of his legs rising upward, striking the ball with an ankle stone. The ball sprang into the air toward his mid-court, where it was deftly deflected in the direction of a teammate who further slowed its momentum. With extraordinary skill, the Eagle team's front four players manipulated the ball by way of their bodies and their striking stones. Players were careful not to touch one another unless they were competing for possession of the ball, but when they did make contact, it was violent.

"My gosh," Nicky Neill murmured, "these guys are unbelievable. Two of the Jaguars are hurt...and one is limping badly."

"Watch closely," One-Zero instructed.

At that moment, the two injured Jaguars initiated a guarded withdrawal to the rear as two of their backcourt teammates rushed forward to take their places. With a burst of effort, the four front Eagles raced away from the fresh Jaguars toward the wall nearest them. The Eagle with the mask struck the ball hard, and it caromed like a bullet toward the sloping wall, where it skip-bounced upward and collided with the vertical wall. Every spectator in the stadium leapt to his feet, screaming wildly.

"Dang!" Nicky Neill exclaimed.

The ball blasted off the wall, but another player's body absorbed the powerful blow. As the man fell backward, he tapped the ball with an ankle stone. For an instant, the lively sphere appeared to achieve inertia, and in that split second another Eagle sprang off the sloping wall and rapped the ball with his elbow. It rebounded off the stone face and struck the scoring ring mere inches off center. A collective groan echoed above the crowd as the ball plummeted. The Eagle leader, however, anticipated this outcome. On the ball's second bounce, he struck it with his ankle stone, sending it soaring downfield.

"Mayan competitors soar gracefully in the ancient ball game"

The entire Eagle mid-court crew had already raced to their opposition's end zone. When the ball touched down, the two injured players were overpowered and watched helplessly as the Eagles gained control of the ball and sent it flying into the end zone, where it struck the ground and skittered to the back wall. The stadium erupted in a thunder crack of approval. The first point had been tallied.

"Wow!" Nicky Neill exclaimed. "I see that this is a battle after all."

"Hmm." One-Zero nodded in response. "Pretty much."

CHAPTER 53

"We came here for your father," One-Zero said. "I'm pleased to see that he's not in this stadium."

"That's a good thing?"

"Yes, it's a very good thing. Not to mention that having pretty much the entire city wrapped up in the Ball Game makes our trespassing a tad less perilous."

"Yeah," Nicky Neill glanced back at the ball court, "if they're not in that stadium, they're drunk or asleep. Right?"

"Hmm. That's a safe bet in regards to the rank and file. But soldiers and warriors will be at their duty stations, and they're the ones we have to avoid."

"Right. Let's get on with this."

Nicky Neill began the long, slow crawl from the roof's summit to the eave below. One-Zero kept pace beside him. When they reached the lower edge, they crept to the building's corner. Nicky Neill was the first to descend. When his feet touched the cobblestone alleyway, he scooted into the shadows cast by the adjacent structure.

"Okay!" he hissed. "I'm clear."

One-Zero rose from his crouched position and surveyed the narrow tunnel two stories below. Then he jumped.

"Aww-hh!" Nicky Neill gasped in horror and bolted forward to render aid. But his friend touched down upon the stone path without making a sound.

One-Zero calmly turned to the boy. "Remind me to teach you that trick sometime. It comes in handy now and again."

Nicky Neill shook his head in near disbelief. "You don't surprise me so much anymore, One-Zero, but I have to admit, you always amaze me."

Keeping to the shadows as much as possible, the pair made their way down a labyrinth of alleys and footpaths before their trail began to rise.

"We're heading for the ceremonial complex, aren't we?" Nicky Neill asked.

"Right," One-Zero responded. "We should be approaching the causeway that links the city to the great plaza."

They pressed on in silence. In the course of their trek, they had not encountered another soul. Fate appeared to be on their side.

"Whoa! There's the causeway, just up ahead." One-Zero gestured. "See it?"

"Yes, sir, I see it." The arc of a bridge caused the trail in the near distance to buckle. "That's our gateway, right?"

One-Zero stared hard in the direction of the overpass. "We have company," he said at last. "There's a group of soldiers on the far side, guards I assume. I can't say how many for certain, but I detect at least five or six distinct voices."

"So, what's our move? Circle 'round to the back door?"

"There ain't one." One-Zero continued to stare ahead. "The ceremonial plaza is an island, completely set apart from the rest of the city. And this bridge is the only way in or out."

"So, how do we solve this puzzle?"

"Ah." One-Zero slumped to a sitting position, his back supported by a smooth stone wall. "We wait."

"Wait? Are you kidding me?" Nicky Neill looked at his partner resting comfortably against the embankment. "Don't you have a special plan for this kind of thing?"

"Sit, little brother." One-Zero patted the hard surface. "I've got the jumpin' thing down to an art, but I'm still workin' on the flyin' part."

CHAPTER 54

*N*icky Neill leaned into the darkened shadows and listened intently before he returned to the mountainous wall and slouched down next to his friend.

"You're right," he sighed. "There's six of them. Too many for your blowgun, huh?"

"Yep, that's a fact." One-Zero took in a long, deep breath, held it, and then exhaled slowly.

"What are you doing, One-Zero?"

"Deep breathing," he responded. "Lookin' for a way over that bridge."

"Ah, I knew you were working on it!" Nicky Neill felt a flood of relief sweep over his body. There was nothing to be done but wait and think. He closed his eyes. There was no way, he thought, that he could fall asleep...no way at all.

The next conscious thought Nicky Neill had was that of a rooster's crow. "Huh?" He bolted upright and struggled to open and focus his eyes at the same time. His immediate world was still cloaked in darkness, but faint veins of pink and orange were streaking across the sky over his shoulder. "Oh, my gosh! One-Zero, look! It's..."

One-Zero was not beside him. To Nicky Neill's dismay, his friend had vanished.

"I hate it when he does this," Nicky Neill murmured to himself. He rolled to one side and pushed himself up and away from the wall, but his feet caused him to collapse back to the stone mattress that had hosted his fitful nap. "What the heck!" With great tenderness he explored the soles of his feet. The skin on the bottoms of both of them was raw, cracked, and caked with dried blood. "Oh, man," he moaned. "Not good...not good." Then something hard and cold collided with his right leg. "Aggh! What the—?"

"Jumpy, huh?" One-Zero called out softly from the shadows.

"Holy cow, One-Zero! I'm too young to go out with a heart attack. Where have you been, and what did you drop on me?"

"Take a look. What you find will explain everything."

Nicky Neill groped the surface beside his right leg. His fingers collided with a foreign object. It was roundish, the size of a grapefruit, and both hard and soft at the same time.

"Is this breakfast? Or are we going to lob fruit bombs at those guards across the way?"

"Bounce it," One-Zero directed. "But be ready."

Nicky Neill hoisted the object to chest level and released it between his legs. In an instant, it ricocheted off the stone and slammed into his chin, rattling his teeth in the process.

"Dang! It's a ball! It's one of the balls from the game. How the heck did you get your hands on this?"

"Deep breathing," One-Zero replied. "We gotta move, pard. You heard that rooster crow."

"Yeah, I heard it. It won't be dark for much longer. What's the plan?"

"Well, before I lay out my scheme, try these on." One-Zero dropped a clumsy bundle on Nicky Neill's lap.

"Sandals!" Nicky Neill looked up at One-Zero. "Just before you showed up, I was rubbing the bottoms of my feet. They're a mess, man."

"Yeah, I figured as much. Try 'em on." The outline of One-Zero's face began to take shape in the creeping dawn.

Nicky Neill slipped into the sandals and adjusted the leather strapping. Then he stood up and paced about their hiding niche. "*¡Gracias a Diós!*" he exclaimed. "They fit! Hallelujah! You saved me, man!"

"Good, let's get on with this game." One-Zero edged around Nicky Neill and assumed a crouching position. Keeping low, he scurried to the causeway. Nicky Neill was close on his heels. At the crest of the rise, they stopped.

"Got that ball?" One-Zero held out an open palm.

"Yes, sir. Here it is." He placed the mysterious sphere in his friend's grasp. Then he crowded closer to see what One-Zero had cooked up.

One-Zero placed the ball in the middle of the bridge and gave it a gentle nudge. It immediately disappeared into the shadows.

"That's it?" Nicky Neill muttered under his breath. "Roll the ball at them?"

One-Zero did not respond. He was waiting for something when a cry went up on the other end of the bridge, followed by excited shouting.

"Now," One-Zero turned to Nicky Neill, "we move fast and not a sound, right? We slip past these boys and we're on our way."

"But what's keeping them from stopping us? I don't get it."

"If somebody tossed a football to you and a bunch of your buddies back home, what would you do?" One-Zero's face was clearly revealed in the early sunlight. He was grinning from ear to ear. "Are you with me?"

"Yeah. All the way."

CHAPTER 55

*A*t the crest of the causeway, they paused to check things out. The span ahead of them was empty. Somewhere beyond the portal to the ceremonial complex, voices could be heard.

"They're going at it, aren't they?"

"They sure are." One-Zero nodded. "Boys will be boys." Just then, an agonizing scream rose above the clamor. "Hmm," he sighed. "And that ball will be true to its own disposition."

Keeping low, they hustled over the remaining distance. At the base of a great arch, they discovered an arsenal of weapons strewn upon the ground.

"What's this?" Nicky Neill toed a long spear nestled in a notched slab of carved hardwood.

"Atlatl." One-Zero raised his eyebrows in recognition. "Increases the range. This way," he pointed, "away from the action."

The pair dashed through the archway and angled left, running along a broad lane. In less than a hundred yards, the passage emptied into a slender plateau that fronted a complex of temples. On the other side of the plateau, their path narrowed into a steep incline, a route that wound past a compound of impressive two-story dwellings.

"Apartments," One-Zero pointed out, "for priests and nobles." Nicky Neill was too winded to respond.

Before long, they arrived at the top of the ramp and were confronted by a high wall.

"We have to split up for a bit, pard." One-Zero looked into Nicky Neill's face. Daylight was flooding the upper reaches of the city, and only a thin shroud of darkness remained.

"We're looking for a door, right?" Nicky Neill replied.

"Or a hole in the wall! If one of us finds an opening, call out like a whippoorwill." With that, One-Zero spun away and loped down the wall to the left of their position.

Nicky Neill set off to his right. He hadn't covered fifty paces when he heard his favorite Oklahoma sound. He turned on a dime and raced in the opposite direction. He found One-Zero standing in front of a tall wooden gate.

"Now what?" Nicky Neill shrugged his shoulders. "You haven't opened it already?"

"You get that honor."

Nicky Neill raised one hand, pressed it against the door, and gave it a shove. It did not budge. He laid both hands against it and tried again. Still nothing. With frustration mounting, he slammed his shoulder into it and the great wooden slab groaned and gave way a few feet. Nicky Neill poked his head through and spied a catwalk disappearing around a corner to his left. "All clear," he signaled.

"Okay," One-Zero whispered as he eased beyond the gate. "Easy does it now. We're close to where we want to be."

Together, they approached the narrow walkway attached to the backside of an unrecognizable structure. Nicky Neill took the lead and set off down the ramp, treading cautiously as they found themselves enveloped in darkness once again. Soon their path made a right angle. Warily, Nicky Neill navigated the turn. He was confronted by the trail's end.

CHAPTER 56

*F*rom where Nicky Neill stood, there remained four feet of trail and wall. Beyond that a broad expanse of intricately laid stone stretched across an immense courtyard bounded on all sides by enormous ceremonial structures. Plumes of gray smoke trailed into the early morning sky. One pyramid towered above all the others. It was so massive it cast a shadow across the entire quadrangle. Nicky Neill crept to the end of the catwalk and peered upward.

"Aggh!" he gasped.

"Yep," One-Zero nudged his companion, "that's our destination."

"Dang! It's huge!" Nicky Neill turned to One-Zero. Even in the soft shadows of dawn, it was clear that the color had drained from his face. "My dad's inside that monster."

"A platoon of soldiers are stationed at the courtyard two-thirds of the way up, in the center of this giant. Where they put your pap on display."

Nicky Neill nodded in recollection.

"We've got to move fast before the opportunity passes."

"I'm ready. How do we do this?"

"Listen close. And do precisely what I tell you. Don't ask any questions. There's no time."

"Yes, sir, I understand."

"Failure is not an option," One-Zero began. "You've got to get past the guards first, including one or more at the door to your pap's cell. And then you have to unlock the pyramid. Once you're inside, there may be more than one tunnel leading to his chamber. Plus, it'll be black as coal in there. And," he added, "your pap may not be the only prisoner."

One-Zero cut short his explanation when a hint of terror registered in Nicky Neill's expression.

"Son, you won't be entirely alone. I'm gonna help ya. This operation requires the two of us: me out here and you on the inside. ¿Entiendes?"

"Sí."

"Okay, good. I'm confident with my part," he went on, "but your piece will be extremely difficult. In fact, the outcome is pretty much ridin' on you."

"You know...I...well, me and Ploox, we've been tackling the unknown ever since we left home. So, I'll tell you right now, One-Zero, you keep laying out what I have to do and I'll do it. Just please, drop the extreme part 'cause, to tell you the truth, none of this should be close to possible!"

"Point taken," One-Zero acknowledged. "All right, I'm going to project an image, a mental image so powerful that every livin' thing within a hundred yards will be incapacitated, immobilized...and so will you unless you do exactly as I say."

Nicky Neill nodded.

"I'm going to take you by the shoulders and turn you around. When I do that, I want you to close your eyes and create a picture in your mind. I want you to envision an image of a burnin' candle. Focus on that candle. Blot out everything else. You must concentrate so hard that you feel the heat from its solitary flame. Then, as I push you off, extend the candle through your mind into the real world. Send it out an arm's length in front of your nose and keep it there. No matter what you encounter, do not allow that flame to go out or disappear. Understand?"

Nicky Neill nodded again.

"That candle will be your guide and your protection. If you lose it, you will lose your ability to act and we'll be finished here." One-Zero placed a light hand on Nicky Neill's shoulder. "There is nothin' in this world, at this moment, so important to you as this candle. Are you ready?"

"Yes." Nicky Neill's response was no more than a murmur.

"All right, amigo. Your father believes in you. And I believe in you. Bring him out!"

One-Zero's light touch transformed into a viselike grip. His other hand fell upon the boy's shoulder, and it, too, clamped down with a vengeance. Time stood still. Nicky Neill closed his eyes. An image of a burning candle materialized in his mind. It was suspended in the center of a rapidly expanding mental space. Its yellow flame burned brightly, unwaveringly. One-Zero began to turn him around. As he turned, Nicky Neill concentrated on the candle. He had never in his life focused so hard on a single thing. One-Zero released his grip and gently pushed his friend ahead.

Nicky Neill began to move forward like a child taking his first steps. In the beginning, everything outside his head was black. There was no pyramid, no stone beneath his feet, nothing except the burning candle occupying the center of his attention.

CHAPTER 57

Several paces into his launch, Nicky Neill stopped. The candle in his head had begun to vibrate. A mounting sense of panic swelled at the base of his spine. Through force of will he remained focused on the candle. As he recaptured his self-control, the tiny flame passed through his forehead into the world.

Outside images reappeared, but only in a peripheral sense. It was as if he were riding his bike back home, staring at the street ahead yet still aware of things on either side. He continued to move forward, and as he did he perceived a strange, sharp ringing in his ears.

Although Nicky Neill's attention was riveted on the candle, he maintained the ability to interact with the world. He stood at the base of the great pyramid. He mounted the first step cautiously, balancing the candle as he climbed. Each successive step required the same degree of attention. His ascent followed this precise pattern until an image formed in the near distance above him.

With two more steps the image took shape. It was a Mayan soldier. He appeared fierce, angry. The expression tattooed upon his face pierced Nicky Neill's imagination, and for a millisecond the candle's flame flickered and grew dim. He struggled to regain his composure and redirect his attention. As he did the candle's shape clarified and the glow returned to its former brilliance. He vowed not to be unsettled again. After all, the soldier was immobile, somehow transformed into living stone. With great care he guided himself around the Mayan and set about finding the door that would lead to his father's cell.

He recalled precisely the route and the number of steps the two soldiers had taken to retrieve his dad. Upon mounting the seventeenth stair above the plaza level, he confronted a door. A triangular shape stood out in an odd cleft where three steps should have been. His heart began to race. He repeated One-Zero's advice. "Focus on the candle." The rushing blood subsided and his heartbeat almost returned to normal. With his left hand he began skimming the surface of the door. "Ah-hah!" he gasped. His fingers slid into a rectangular slot. "A keyhole? But where's the key?" He felt the initial stage of panic course through his body again, but he kept it at bay. The candle's flame was strong; he was okay. He lifted his right hand and brought it to bear in the exploration of the door. But there was no key, no tool dangling on a nail to insert in the slot. Two fingers from his right hand revisited the keyhole. Mouthing a plea, he pushed his fingers into the notch with all the force he could muster.

A small explosion erupted within the door, followed by a blast of cold air as the triangle of stone separated from the niche and swung outward.

"Whoa! What the heck!" he exclaimed, scooting backward to avoid an impact with the massive slab rushing toward him. Then it stopped. Like the gaping mouth of some long-sleeping monster, the opening yawned before him. It was dark and smelled of rotten eggs.

Nicky Neill stepped forward and peered into the blackness. As he did, his candle illuminated a narrow stairwell that angled downward. Every hair on the back of his neck sprang to attention and quivered with anticipation. His dad was only yards away, and he was going to find him. With trembling feet, he set off down the stairway, following the course blazed by the candle's beam.

CHAPTER 58

*T*he steps inside the pyramid were smaller than those on the exterior, and the stairwell was narrow. As Nicky Neill negotiated the tight, foul passage, the walls began to close in around him and his breathing became labored. The candle's flame started to waver, then flicker.

"No! No!" he gasped. He arrested his descent. His entire body was trembling. He forced all thoughts from his mind and stared hard at the still-quivering plume of fire. Gradually, the flame's fluttering ceased.

"Whew! Okay, okay, I'm good." Nicky Neill's whispered relief trailed into the shadows behind him as he renewed his downward progress.

Some thirty steps further the tight corridor split. One set of stairs angled to his left, another wound off to his right. Nicky Neill lingered and waited for a sign. Seconds later, the candle's flame tilted toward the right. He veered in that direction and continued on. Forty more steeply declining steps delivered him to a doorway of sorts. In actuality, the size of the passageway merely expanded into a cavern. Nicky Neill's feet welcomed the flat surface of a true floor. In a matter of seconds, he crossed the room and encountered a wall.

"Huh? This is it?" He began to pace the chamber, searching for another door or staircase. Instead, he encountered only more wall. He would have to retrace his steps and explore the other passage. As he groped toward the exit, he stumbled over something.

"What?" He jammed the toe of one of his sandals into the object. Whatever he was nudging, it was soft. He lowered himself to a kneeling position and surveyed the floor. He discovered an untidy mound of rags and blankets strewn across the cold stone. He stood up again and kicked at the pile of refuse. To his surprise, his foot struck something solid. He kicked at the lump again, exploring the contour of it with successive raps. Once again, he knelt close to the floor. This time he employed his hands and those sensitive, cave-trained fingers. While he combed through the clump of material, he kept his gaze focused on the candle. Its golden flame continued to glow an arm's length beyond his nose.

"Here! What's this?" Nicky Neill's fingers made contact with a solid object. At first, he drew back from his discovery. Then he grasped it and pulled it toward him. But it resisted. He dug deeper, seeking a better handhold. There, he had it. Both hands clutched securely onto a...a shoulder!

"Aggh!" Nicky Neill pulled away, as if recoiling from a snakebite. His heart exploded inside his chest. The candle began to rock from side to side in the near distance. His head started to spin and his entire body became numb. "No! No! I can't lose it, not now!" He urged himself to recover, to regain control of the situation. If he imploded, everything would crash. They would all be goners.

He moved back in and began stripping away at the layers of rags and blankets that formed a cocoon-like cover for the body on the floor. Then another thought pierced his brain. What if the body he was toiling to unwrap was not a body at all? What if it was a corpse? That theory was followed by another: what if the person beneath him was not his dad at all?

With trembling fingers, he continued at his task. As the last layers of material peeled away, a human form took shape. Nicky Neill tugged at a coil of cloth twisted around the figure's shoulders and laid it aside. The body was posed on its side, with its back to its unraveller. Nicky Neill took a deep breath, stared hard at the candle's yellow radiance, and then gave the body a solid heave, flipping it over onto its back.

With a lump in his throat, he moved in even closer to the inert form. Still, there was no recognition. He guided his candle to a point on the floor beside a disheveled head of hair.

Seconds passed, followed closely by an eternity of disbelief and then, rapture.

"Dad!...Dad! It's you!"

CHAPTER 59

*N*icky Neill staggered on his haunches and fell backward. An avalanche of events and places and faces stormed across his mind's eye. But a tiny flame, wavering erratically in the darkness, redelivered him to the task at hand.

"Dad! Dad! You need to get up. We have to get out of here. Now!" Dr. Carpenter's body appeared lifeless. Nicky Neill applied two fingers to the carotid artery in his father's neck. He detected a pulse, faint but present. He was paralyzed, just like the Mayan soldier at his post. Seized with a growing sense of panic, the boy managed to get his father to his feet.

The journey up the passageway was agonizing. Nicky Neill quickly understood the staircase design; weak, disoriented prisoners would not have been able to negotiate taller stairs.

With no notion of the passage of time, Nicky Neill and his father reached the tunnel's end. As they staggered into the fresh air, the boy was gripped by a new sense of alarm. Everywhere across the ceremonial complex, shadows were withdrawing. A legion of roosters labored to bring in the day.

Nicky Neill did not possess the luxury of quelling his alarm. He had the enormous exterior steps of the pyramid to negotiate with his father. And he had to maintain the candle's flame, which had turned pale in the creeping dawn. Without thinking it through, Nicky Neill leaned into his father's body and twisted beneath him so that his comatose accomplice was draped across his back like a lumpy blanket. The boy clasped his passenger's hands together and laced the fingers of each hand. In that fashion, the pair made their way down the pyramid. Nicky Neill barely noticed the fierce soldier still frozen at his post as he slid past him.

At the base of the pyramid, Nicky Neill eased his father from his back and combed the shadows that still lingered along the catwalk where he had left One-Zero. He was not hard to find. His friend was leaning against the stone, immersed in the trance that he had generated.

Nicky Neill pulled his father to his feet and quasi-dragged him toward the catwalk. As they approached One-Zero, he raised his head but his eyes remained sealed. When they drew alongside him, his hand shot up and a thumb extended, pointing down-trail.

Nicky Neill tightened his grip around his dad's waist and quickened their pace. Their speed increased as the path began its downward run. Moments later they reached the heavy gate below. Nicky Neill wedged half his body in the open space and leaned hard against the wooden slab. The door groaned and swung out enough for the pair to slip through. Nicky Neill opened his eyes and the candle's image evaporated. The world came into clear focus.

The narrow plaza they lurched through gave way to the broad lane that in turn led to the causeway. There were still no guards in sight. Nicky Neill gasped as they rounded a corner and the bridge became visible. The incessant crowing that continued to erupt from every quarter of the city was now accompanied by a chorus of yelping dogs. "Oh, my gosh!" Nicky Neill muttered beneath labored breath. "This whole place is waking up."

"Oooh!" Dr. Carpenter stirred and groaned at his son's side. "My head is killing me! Where am I?"

"Dad! You're awake! It's me, Nicky Neill!"

"What?" He yawned and struggled to open his eyes. "Sticky what did you say?" Then he stumbled backward a half step, only to catch himself and realign his body into a fully upright position. As if bludgeoned by a lightning bolt, he threw himself at the stranger beside him, sobbing, laughing, and gasping, uncontrollably. "How? How?"

"It's me, Dad! It's definitely me; you're not dreaming!" Nicky Neill was surprised by the strength of the embrace. "Dad, we don't have time right now for me to explain everything. I have a friend, a powerful friend, who's helping me. We're taking you out of here but we've got to move..."

Wheeew-wheet! A sharp whistle pierced the relative calm.

"There!" Nicky Neill twisted his head around and peered over his shoulder. "That's him!"

One-Zero was sprinting over the cobblestone like an Olympic champion. To Dr. Carpenter, however, the figure in the closing distance appeared as a floating blanket with legs. He did recognize an arm extended above the blanket, gesturing emphatically that they get a move on.

"Your friend is a blanket?" he exclaimed.

"Yep, at the moment he is. Let's go, Dad!"

$\mathcal{N}$icky Neill pulled his father's arm over his shoulder and locked his grip onto a frail wrist. His other hand snaked around his dad's waist, securing a hold through an empty belt loop.

"We've got to fly, Dad! Stay with me as best you can." Nicky Neill lurched forward, dragging his father beside him. But Dr. Carpenter quickly found his footing and began to move under his own power.

"Nobody ever beat us in the sack race, Nick!" he grunted. "We've still got the rhythm!"

"Hah! You're right, Dad. Keep telling yourself that!"

The pair rushed onto the bridge with a full head of steam. At the top of the rise, they listed. As if trapped in slow motion,

"The rescuers and the escapee flee into the night"

Nicky Neill felt them lean, then career, toward the railing. Dr. Carpenter hit it first, then a second time as Nicky Neill slammed into him. For an instant they teetered on the lip of the structure, unable to pull back. In that moment, a viselike grip yanked them back onto the middle of the bridge.

"That ain't the shortcut we're lookin' for!" One-Zero's chest was heaving as he spoke. "We'll talk later, Doc. Now, git!" He centered them on the span and pushed them forward with a powerful heave.

Seconds later, the trio spilled off the bridge and continued their race into the heart of the city. As they ran, Nicky Neill detected a strange sound in the distance behind them. The sound soon became a distinct noise, a swelling buzz that echoed commotion. Then, high overhead, a brittle scream erupted. Jaguar Man was exhorting their capture and death. The growing cacophony of rabid voices and a waking city encouraged the escapees to push even harder.

At the end of the murky alleyway, the great depression that housed the ball court loomed into view.

"What now, One-Zero?" Nicky Neill pressed his father into a thin curtain of shadows that still clung to the row of buildings lining their path.

"Retrace our steps from last night...that will lead to the only exit we know of for sure." One-Zero studied his companions. "Dr. Carpenter, are you able to continue with Nicky Neill's help?"

"Yes. Yes, thank you." Dr. Carpenter labored to speak as he gasped for breath. Then he added, "I...have...an idea...that might...help us!"

"What, Dad? What have you got?" Nicky Neill turned back to his father.

"If we stay...above ground...our risks will only increase. I think I know...of a shortcut, a real one."

One-Zero wrinkled his brow. "Do share, sir."

"The Mayans have constructed runoff tunnels throughout the city; they empty into the river. I believe they might be large enough to accommodate us."

"Can you locate one of these tunnels, Professor?"

"Yes, I think I can." Dr. Carpenter was still breathing hard, but his speech was no longer labored.

"Then let's find it, Dad!" Nicky Neill tightened his grip on his father. "And fast."

"This way." The professor gestured, pointing toward an intersecting alley. He stepped forward on his own and pushed off from his son's grasp. His gait was wobbly, punctuated by a significant limp, but he picked up speed with each stride.

Their course kept to the same alley, a fact that made Nicky Neill nervous. Still, he held his tongue in check. Every thirty yards their path intersected with a wider street. At each junction, Dr. Carpenter paused and searched for signs of a runoff. As they raced toward the next intersection, he screeched to a halt. Nicky Neill plowed into him from behind.

"What, Dad? What is it?"

Ahead of them, a high wall blocked their path.

"What now?" Nicky Neill's head swiveled frantically in search of an alternate route.

"Down there!" Dr. Carpenter gestured to his right. "Our best hope is to parallel the wall. This narrowing is a natural drainage course."

"Take the lead, Doctor." One-Zero nodded in agreement. "Nick, I'll bring up the rear. And," he added, "pay attention to what he won't be lookin' for."

Dr. Carpenter set off down the narrow channel with his two accomplices close behind him.

For the first time since their dash over the causeway, they were completely exposed. There were no shadows cast beneath the wall, no lingering pockets of darkness as yet unburned by the morning sun. They stood out like jail breakers silhouetted in a spotlight's beam.

Almost immediately, a commotion ignited over their shoulders. Nicky Neill recognized the war cries of soldiers, the same fierce shrieking he and Jorge had heard as the Lacandon warriors closed in on them in the forest.

At the bottom of the incline, Dr. Carpenter skidded to a halt. "There!" He pointed. "Everything empties there!"

They backtracked in a panic and darted down a narrow passageway opposite the wall. Some twenty feet into the opening, they confronted a hump-shaped berm of rammed earth overlaid with stone. A thick, broad slab of rock had been notched into the berm facing out toward the passageway. At the base of the slab, a six-inch slit ran from end to end.

"That would be the duct," Dr. Carpenter said.

"Right." Nicky Neill agreed. "How do we get in there?" Before anyone could offer a clue, a rain of arrows cascaded into the cramped fissure. Most of the missiles slammed into the berm, but several struck the walls and ricocheted wildly. One of the small spears pierced One-Zero's blanket and dangled at his side.

"Stand back!" One-Zero ordered. "And cover your heads as best you can!" He approached the slab and squared off with it. With cat-like agility, he dipped low, grasped the stone at its base, and gave it a mighty yank. The rock squeaked, but it hardly moved.

Nicky Neill pulled his arms from his head and squinted along the passageway. "Dang! They're sliding down the wall! They're coming after us!"

One-Zero did not look up. Instead, he closed his eyes and took a deep breath. Then he leaned away from the slab, pulling on it with every ounce of power he could muster. As he strained, Nicky Neill heard the warriors' footsteps echoing off the cobblestone surface.

The slab registered a harsh, grating noise as it pulled away from the placement. Nicky Neill glanced toward the tight cluster of Mayan warriors now advancing cautiously down the corridor, their weapons at the ready. He made out their forms clearly. There were five of them.

"How do we fight them?" Nicky Neill looked to One-Zero.

"We don't!" he barked. "Squeeze through this crack, quickly!" A ten-inch gap loomed in the recess where the stone cover had been torn away.

Nicky Neill pushed his father toward the gash. "Hurry, Dad, get in!" With surprising agility, Dr. Carpenter threw himself at the space and wriggled into the void. Nicky Neill followed after him. Together they scurried deeper into the shaft. Almost immediately, the duct narrowed into a three-foot by three-foot chute. "Holy cow!" Nicky Neill murmured. "If it gets any smaller, we'll be in a real pickle."

"Where's your friend? I haven't seen him squeeze in yet."

"Cripes! He's still out there!" Nicky Neill pulled away from his father and scrambled back to the unattended fissure.

As soon as Nicky Neill's head edged through the opening, he heard the sounds of a fierce struggle echoing off the walls of the narrow portal. In a split second he was clear of the crack and stumbling over One-Zero's pouch. "What the—?" The raging scene that played out at the far end of the corridor blunted his surprise.

One-Zero's bare back glistened in the misty yellow light. His blanket now covered his entire left arm, which he used as a shield. His right hand flashed through the haze, again and again. Nicky Neill recognized the telescope in his grasp. A knot of warriors fought back, wielding their clubs like a single buzz saw. Nicky Neill had never witnessed a life-or-death struggle before. Shaken by the cries that accompanied the battle, he scooped up One-Zero's pouch and threw open the flap. A slender bundle riveted his attention. He jerked it clear of the bag and shook it until it unraveled. One-Zero's blowgun tumbled to his feet, followed by a cluster of wicked darts. With trembling hands he managed to extend the telescopic tube to its full length. Still shaking, he pushed a dart into the breech, scooped up the rest of the barbs, and raced down the channel toward the brawl.

The stone path at One-Zero's feet was drenched in blood. Gashes in both of his shoulders bled profusely, and his head and neck were awash in crimson sweat.

Nicky Neill fell to his knees less than a yard behind his friend and forced a burst of air into the weapon's mouthpiece.

In a matter of seconds, a warrior collapsed on the floor, eyeball to eyeball with his assailant. The soldier's eyes were filled with rage but he could not blink. Nicky Neill chambered another dart and sent it flying into the fray. A second warrior collapsed onto his fallen comrade.

"Give me a dart!" One-Zero shouted. "In my hand!" Nicky Neill slammed a tiny arrow into his friend's open palm. "Another!" he barked. Two more Mayans crumpled to the surface.

"That's it!" Nicky Neill called back. "We're out!"

"No matter." One-Zero faced off with a lone warrior. A shriek erupted from the Mayan's throat before he charged at the giant in his path. His blood-spattered war club struck One-Zero's forearm. The weapon's blade snared in the coarse fabric. The last thing he saw was One-Zero's fist rushing toward his face.

One-Zero spun about. "Let's git! Their friends can't be far behind!"

Nicky Neill's mouth fell open. One-Zero's chest and legs bled profusely. A half-dozen arrows protruded from his body. "You won't fit in the crack!" he blurted.

"Break 'em off! Be quick about it!"

Nicky Neill jumped to his feet. He did not think about what he was ordered to do. He just did it. He snapped the brittle shafts of six arrows embedded in One-Zero's flesh.

"Good, well done! Now make for that hole while we still can!" As they scurried toward the berm, the air above them came alive with an ominous whispering sound. One-Zero's body cleared the opening as the first wave of arrows poured into the passage. A second wave followed close behind.

CHAPTER 61

$\mathcal{N}$ icky Neill and his dad scrambled deeper into the tunnel and waited for One-Zero. A muffled noise, of stone grating on stone, reverberated in the near distance. The honey-colored shaft of light that angled into the drainage flue grew thinner and thinner until it disappeared altogether. Seconds later, One-Zero was beside them.

"Reinforcements are on the way! What are we faced with here?"

"It narrows down," Nicky Neill responded. "We'll have to crawl."

One-Zero dropped his bag at his feet and probed its contents. "Ah!" he muttered. "Hold this, Nick." He thrust a small, cylindrical object into Nicky Neill's hand. Then a match ignited and burst into flame. "Raise the lid."

Nicky Neill pulled back a glass cover that sheltered a small candle. One-Zero applied the blazing match to the exposed wick. "There! It's good!" Nicky Neill returned the cover. "Dang, One-Zero, what do you not have in that saddlebag?"

"We've got company!" Dr. Carpenter announced. An escalating commotion was unfolding on the opposite side of the slab.

"Take us down, pard. They'll be in here with us before we know it!"

Nicky Neill took the lead, moving as quickly as he could on three limbs, holding the lantern aloft before him. For the first hundred feet, the drainage duct angled downward at a gentle slope before it began a steep descent. In a heartbeat, Nicky Neill lost control of his pace. His feet flew away from him and he plummeted haphazardly through empty air.

"Ugh!" He grimaced upon impact.

Dr. Carpenter crashed to the ground seconds behind his son.

"Wha—!" he exclaimed. His surprise was cut short by the bulk of One-Zero's body plowing into him like a battering ram. "Agh!"

"Sorry, Doc! Are you okay, sir?"

"I'm fine, I'm all right. Thank you. What did we encounter?"

"It's a screen," One-Zero answered, exploring the object with both hands. "A bamboo lattice, and a stout one at that."

"Why is it here?" Nicky Neill pushed an arm through an opening in the mesh. "Hey! I think this is the end of the tunnel. I hear water running somewhere below us."

"Hmm, I reckon this is a device to keep curious Mayan children from fallin' into the river. Ah-hah!" One-Zero withdrew a slender blade embedded in a wooden handle from his pouch. "We, however, need to make that tumble." He applied the edge of his tool to the midsection of the framework and began to saw with a vengeance.

Nicky Neill crowded closer with the lantern to illuminate his friend's effort. For the first time since he entered the tunnel, Dr. Carpenter got a good look at his son's remarkable companion.

"Oh, my goodness, man! You're injured...seriously!" One-Zero's upper body looked like a pincushion; jagged stubs of broken arrows sprouted across his torso. Blood leaked from every wound and dark fluid seeped from the gashes in his shoulders.

"The water will stop the bleedin'," he acknowledged. "And I have a friend who's good at patchin' people up."

"But, One-Zero," Nicky Neill leaned in closer, gawking at the punctures and lacerations, "what about piranhas?"

One-Zero stopped sawing and looked down at Nicky Neill's earnest face. "That would be a concern in the Amazon," he winked, "but not here in the lost world."

CHAPTER 62

"There!" One-Zero's blade broke through the lattice. "One more incision and we're on our way. Nick, while I finish this, plumb my bag for a clump of twine. We should lower our lantern into this hole...it'd be good to know what we're droppin' into."

Nicky Neill located the string and, with the help of his father, tied off to their light source. "Here goes," he announced as he guided the lantern through the grille. All three of the fugitives craned their heads after the candle. "It's not the river," he declared. "It's another tunnel...a much bigger one."

"Good!" One-Zero's hand pierced the barrier a second time. "Pull back!" Nicky Neill and his father pressed themselves against the passage walls while their friend stomped out an expanded opening. "You first, Nick! Take my hand."

Nicky Neill passed the lantern's string to his father and slipped into the ragged slot. He plunged straightaway into thin air. He would have fallen fast had he not been anchored to his friend.

"Okay!" he called out. "Let go!" His words were followed by a resounding splash. "I've got the candle, Dad. Come on down! It's maybe seven or eight feet!"

Dr. Carpenter eased through the gash, aided by One-Zero's iron grip.

"Happy landings, Doc!" One-Zero released his hold and in the next second father and son were reunited in six inches of water.

Dr. Carpenter was followed by One-Zero's bag and then his person.

"This is the collection tunnel, isn't it?" Dr. Carpenter observed.

"Yes, sir. And the current flows this way." A head wag set their new course. "You two move as quick as you can to the discharge point. I'll meet you there."

"Huh?" Nicky Neill spun about. "Where are you going?"

"I'm not going anywhere, little brother. I just want to slow those fellas down who are chasin' after us."

"Come on, Dad! He knows what he's doing." Nicky Neill locked arms with his father. "Run!"

Several minutes later, Nicky Neill and Dr. Carpenter followed a turn in the passageway and were struck head-on by a brilliant column of sunlight.

"Aghh!" both men cried out in unison.

"Stay with me, Dad!" Nicky Neill turned his gaze away from the blinding glare. "We're not there yet."

"Wait, son. Do you smell that? That's smoke! Where's your friend?"

"His name's One-Zero, Dad. And I have no doubt that he's behind the smoke!"

"He's very resourceful, isn't he?" Dr. Carpenter turned away from the blinding light and continued to sniff the air.

"You have no idea. Come on, we have to see what's up there." Nicky Neill tightened his grip on his father's arm and pressed forward toward daylight.

Thirty yards' progress delivered them to an opening blocked by the same sort of bamboo obstruction they had just vanquished. As their eyes adjusted to the sun, they pressed their faces against the barricade and squinted, dumbstruck, beyond the grating.

"Cripes!" Nicky Neill gasped. "It just gets better!"

Beneath them, a steady flow of water emptied through the latticework and tumbled toward the river that snaked a hundred feet below.

"You call that better?" Dr. Carpenter's voice was no more than a whisper. When he spoke again, his tone was stronger but just as incredulous. "You're not a boy anymore, are you, son?"

"I'm still your boy, Dad...just a little...different...and so is Ploox."

Dr. Carpenter stepped away from the bamboo screen and studied his son. "Did you say *Ploox*? As in George Plucowski?"

"Yes, sir, one and the same."

"If we survive this experience, we're going to have a talk, a long talk. Just the two of us."

"Sure, Dad, anytime you like. And by the way," Nicky Neill placed a hand gently upon his father's shoulder, "we are going to survive this. I give you my word."

CHAPTER 63

*T*he rhythmic explosions of water displaced by heavy feet signaled One-Zero's approach. Seconds later, he appeared, rounding the turn in the passageway. Nicky Neill and his father grimaced as their companion's hands flew up to cover his eyes.

"Whoa! I wasn't expecting a freight train!" One-Zero continued to shield his face as he drew alongside his friends. "What'd you discover?"

"The river's down there, all right. Way down there, maybe a hundred feet or more. And, there's another bamboo grate blocking the opening." Nicky Neill paused, weighing his words. "This sucker's bigger and thicker than the last one, too."

"Of course! Ain't that the way! Come on, let's size it up."

They approached the barrier together.

"See what I mean?" Nicky Neill's hands gripped the latticework and attempted to shake it hard. "I know Mayans don't have steel, but this stuff is darned close."

"Listen!" Dr. Carpenter's exclamation was charged with panic. "I hear voices, angry voices! They're in the duct!"

One-Zero pressed his face to the screen. "Look below. They're on the river as well. See the boat? Listen to me closely, fellas." Nicky Neill and Dr. Carpenter crowded against the barrier and studied the river. "There's one way out of this as far as I can tell. When this barricade is down, I'll be the first one in the water. I'm going to flip their canoe. When you see it turn, you jump. Maneuver under the canoe; that's where I'll be. The Maya aren't known for their swimmin' skills, so I doubt they'll be concerned with you two falling out of the sky. *Me entienden?*"

"Yes, sir. We got it." Nicky Neill pulled back from the grille and looked to his friend. "What about this?" He patted the bamboo.

One-Zero winked. "Everything and everybody has a weak spot. And this chunk of bamboo is moldy..." he took a step backward and edged toward the wall..."right here!"

One-Zero dropped into the shallow stream and rolled onto his side, supported by an elbow. In that instant, he began to smash a portion of the lattice with his right foot. Within seconds, a tear appeared. Repeated battering splintered the fibers until a sizeable piece of bamboo at the base of the structure gave way altogether. One-Zero sprang to his feet. "Give me a hand, men!" He locked his grip onto the outer rim beneath the fresh opening. Nicky Neill and his dad followed suit. "Pull! Like your lives depend on it! Ugh! 'Cause they do!"

Nicky Neill was astounded when the rim itself began to pull away from the notches in the wall. Then the entire lattice separated from the breach and toppled forward into the morning air.

"Three things!" One-Zero shouted, backing into the tunnel. "Get a runnin' start, and don't land with your arms spread! And lastly, do not hesitate!" With that, he dashed toward the exit and disappeared.

"Oh, my..." Dr. Carpenter shuddered.

Nicky Neill darted to the opening and watched as One-Zero plummeted, bag and all, through the sun-drenched space. When he hit the water, a spray of mist signaled his impact. He did not resurface. The dozen or so warriors in the war canoe were beside themselves. He could hear them shrieking and shouting. He observed them launch a barrage of arrows and spears into the river. Then the canoe rocked violently and flipped, slinging all of the passengers into the roiling water.

"Son," Dr. Carpenter clasped Nicky Neill's hand and pulled him away from the breach, "I...I can't do this. I have a fear of heights. I've never shared this..."

A buzzing sound flooded the passageway behind them, followed by a flurry of screeching noises as a volley of arrow tips ricocheted off the stone walls behind them.

"Dad!" Nicky Neill laced his fingers through his father's and squeezed his hand with all his strength. "I have a fear of us dying, and my fear trumps yours! Now, run!" Nicky Neill's considerable brawn, coupled with his father's surge of adrenaline, impelled them toward the looming cavity. They ran until there was no floor beneath them. Then gravity embraced them and sucked them down like stones.

CHAPTER 64

$\mathcal{N}$ icky Neill retained his grip on his father's hand even though Dr. Carpenter tried desperately to shake free. Unlike his dad, Nicky Neill's eyes remained open as they fell. He knew that a handful of seconds was all he had to size up the bedlam in the river if they were to have any hope of surviving this leg of their escape.

The onrushing water was littered with flailing swimmers and soldier debris. The war canoe was bigger than Nicky Neill had thought, and it remained capsized. And it was raining arrows. He wondered if the warriors in the runoff chute above were concerned for their comrades fighting for their lives in the dark river below. Then came impact.

Their momentum carried them deep, all the way to the muddy bottom. The force of their collision ripped father and son apart. Nicky Neill groped about frantically for his partner. It was his dad who found him. Familiar hands pushed him from below, launching him toward the surface.

"Agh!" Nicky Neill gasped. "Dad! Dad! Where are you?"

Dr. Carpenter popped into view several feet away, spewing river and gasping for breath.

"Son," he blurted, "that wasn't half bad!"

"We gotta dive, Dad! And come up under the canoe...all right?"

"Right!" Dr. Carpenter instantly disappeared.

When he saw his father vanish, Nicky Neill cast a final glance at the turmoil around him. Then he sucked down a lungful of air and sank beneath the confusion. Dodging the wildly thrashing legs of the Mayan warriors struggling to keep their heads above water, he frog-stroked toward a dark shadow on the surface ahead. As he punched through the remaining few feet of water, a war club crashed against his skull. Bolts of lightning accompanied his descent toward the river bottom.

"No!" he screamed, soundlessly. A hand grasped his tunic's collar and pulled him upward. "No!" he shrieked again. This time his voice echoed just beneath the water's surface. He came up fighting.

"Hey! Hey!" One-Zero admonished. "It's me, Nick!"

"Huh? You!" Nicky Neill reined in his assault on the arm that still held him by the collar. "Who clobbered me with the war club?"

"This is what nailed you." One-Zero guided Nicky Neill's hand to the edge of the canoe. "You whacked yourself."

"Oh. Then, where's Dad?"

"I'm here, son. I'm okay." Dr. Carpenter's voice echoed from the far end of the inverted dugout.

"Hold on to the frame, men." One-Zero came back to the business at hand. "Start kickin'! We've got to move downriver, and fast!"

"Are all the warriors in the water?" Nicky Neill spun about and began kicking for all he was worth.

"No. A couple of 'em are on top of us. We'll shake 'em loose once we get movin'."

"What's our chief concern at this moment?" Dr. Carpenter asked. "Apart from some of these guys joining us, that is?"

"More canoes," One-Zero replied. "We'll be in a genuine pickle if they unleash an armada."

CHAPTER 65

*T*he three escapees kicked hard, aided by a current that grew increasingly strong. All the while, hammer blows resounded off the hull of the dugout, reverberating like hailstones on a barn roof.

"Time for our passengers to take their leave. Those war clubs are more than annoying." One-Zero raised the canoe out of the water and rocked it violently. Frantic shouting erupted overhead, followed by piercing screams.

"Are they drowning?" Nicky Neill called out.

"No, they're not drownin', pard. They're cursin'! And it's very colorful!" One-Zero laughed. "Okay, I'm going to take a quick peek topside. Keep kicking!" With a swish, he ducked under the railing and disappeared. Seconds later, he returned.

"Well?" Nicky Neill demanded. "What's happening out there?"

"They're giving chase. There's a whole army of 'em strung along the bank. And there's four or five boats on our tail in hot pursuit." One-Zero paused to catch his breath. "If we push hard, we can beat 'em to the falls."

"Falls?" Dr. Carpenter joined in. "Did you say falls?"

"I did, Doc. But we won't be going over 'em."

"What, then?"

"We go under."

"And after that?" Nicky Neill's question was posed through clenched teeth. His kicking had taken on a renewed sense of urgency.

"Not a clue," One-Zero replied.

A rain of missiles pelted the canoe. All talking ceased, replaced by grunts of extreme exertion. They had to outdistance the Mayan war boats.

In the heat of their flight, a dull roaring noise began to swell within the bubble beneath the canoe.

"Tell me that's the waterfall!" Nicky Neill called out.

"Spot-on," One-Zero answered.

"When do we leave our shelter?" Dr. Carpenter shouted. "Otherwise, we'll be cornered."

"The steps, right?" Nicky Neill asked. "We have to climb out of here to get to the cave."

"That's not an option now," One-Zero bellowed. "We've got to ride this out. With any luck, the next Mayan you see will be Ploox!"

The roar of the water plunging into the river rose in pitch until it became a continuous explosion. But the mere sound of it was tame compared to the instant it struck the dugout. The canoe was pounded deeper into the stream, leaving six inches or less of breathing space for the passengers below. The noise was deafening. Then it stopped. An eerie silence enveloped them. All light vanished.

"Dang!" Nicky Neill exclaimed. "Are we better or worse off?"

"We're beyond the waterfall, that's clear." Dr. Carpenter's voice was almost serene. "But where, exactly, does that leave us?"

"Well," One-Zero responded, "my advice is to hang on tight and keep kicking. If we're lucky we'll come out in one piece somewhere else."

"You mean we're going under, right?" Nicky Neill sighed. "Under the mountain? I guess there's no use to panic. Any more advice?"

"Hah! Just one piece." One-Zero cleared his throat. "Don't leave this bubble, unless you've morphed into an amphibian!"

For a moment, tranquility prevailed. Then the canoe pitched sharply and slammed into a nosedive.

The boat's floor whacked a trio of heads in unison. For Nicky Neill, starlight glimmered briefly then disappeared. There was no more opportunity for thought after that. They were vacuumed into a subterranean roller coaster, one that offered no safety belts or brakes.

CHAPTER 66

*T*he water became icy cold and numbness set in. Nicky Neill experienced the feeling that his body was disappearing. It would be a better death, he thought, than Mayan spears and arrows. His hands were locked on to the railings of the boat and they were determined not to release themselves. And then he envisioned his dad, weakened by weeks of captivity.

"Dad!" He meant it to be a scream, but it came out as a squeaky yelp.

"Son! I'm making it. How are you?"

Nicky Neill was unable to hear his father's last words. A nerve-wracking, sucking sound was followed by another bullet-like plunge, pulling them further beneath the earth. Then their weird and frightening descent took an abrupt twist. In a matter of seconds the water went from near freezing to tepid, then warm and warmer, then hot and directly into near scalding.

"Holy cow!" Nicky Neill crowed. "What the heck is going on?"

"Must be a volcanic tube close by," One-Zero said. "Good for the pores, I'm sure!"

"No kidding!" Nicky Neill replied. "Hey, do you have any idea where this is going?"

"Pretty much. This river resurfaces on the other side of the mountain, not far from the forbidden bridge."

"How do you know all..." Nicky Neill's question was cut short by a vicious collision with an immovable object. The dugout recovered and spun about, only to slam into another barrier. This time it lodged itself in place.

"Hold tight!" One-Zero's voice boomed inside the bubble. "I have to dislodge us...whatever happens, do not leave the boat. Clear?"

"Yes!" Nicky Neill shouted back.

"Right," Dr. Carpenter added.

There was no sound to indicate that One-Zero had left the canoe, but a curious rasping noise near the bow was followed by a burst of start-stop movements as the entire dugout hiccupped in place. Then the boat broke free and began to spin sideways..

"One-Zero! One-Zero!" Nicky Neill cried out. There was no response. "One...!" his words disappeared into his throat as the spinning intensified.

"We're going up!" Dr. Carpenter called out. "Hold tight, Nick!"

The water temperature dropped as they spiraled upward. All sense of direction abandoned the two passengers. Then the boat slammed into another barrier and stopped moving altogether.

"Ughhh...umm...Dad? I can't stop spinning...and it's getting harder to breathe."

Dr. Carpenter moved closer to his son. "I'm...having...a similar experience. I'm afraid...umnft...our oxygen is about to be depleted."

"We've got to find One-Zero...we can't go on without him." Before his father could respond, Nicky Neill drew in a precious breath of air and slipped beneath the canoe.

"Son! No! Come back!" Dr. Carpenter moved to the spot where Nicky Neill had exited the bubble, but was surprised when he collided with a knot of bodies. "What?"

"Stick tight, Doc! I got your boy." One-Zero surfaced inside the canoe, gasping for breath.

"I'm here, Dad! I found him! Or he found me, I'm not sure which."

"Listen close. We have to leave this bubble now. I've seen a green haze beyond us; I'm sure it's daylight. On the count of three, pull in all the air you can muster, then follow me. We're almost out of this. Okay? One-two-three!" One-Zero gulped a piddling mouthful of oxygen and pushed away from the boat. Nicky Neill and Dr. Carpenter followed suit.

Nicky Neill could not tell if the grassy hue in the distance was a hallucination or an oxygen alarm going off in his brain. He decided it really didn't matter because he was with his dad and whatever came next, they would be together.

CHAPTER 67

*N*icky Neill propelled himself toward the patch of light in the distance. The luminescence had gone from green to orange to a pale yellow. Then One-Zero's hand latched onto his wrist and catapulted him upward. Seconds later, his head broke water.

"Oh!...Oh!...Dang!" he gasped as he coughed and sputtered. "Where's Dad?"

"Here, son!" Dr. Carpenter wheezed behind him. "I'm here."

"This way." One-Zero's voice was restrained. "Hold the talkin', fellas." Without so much as a splash, he glided through the water into a slender band of shade that fell beneath a time-worn structure.

"The forbidden bridge?" Nicky Neill whispered, moving into the shadows beside his friend.

One-Zero nodded.

"I know this bridge." Dr. Carpenter's words were barely audible.

The three anchored themselves to the bank and caught their breath. In the distance, the sounds of a disturbance became increasingly clear.

One-Zero let out a short sigh. "The village is a hornet's nest. Look that way," he motioned. "There's plenty of smoke in the sky. We can count on a heap of Lacandon at the river just around the bend, haulin' water. It appears Hector did his job."

"Who's Hector?" Dr. Carpenter interrupted.

"He's a friend, Dad," Nicky Neill replied. "He helped Ploox escape. By now, Ploox ought to be..."

"Ploox?" Dr. Carpenter was confused. "Where is George in all of this?"

"No time for that now, sir." One-Zero began to pull himself from the water. "We have to slip out of here pronto and proceed with our escape. We're not home yet."

"What do we need to do?" Nicky Neill asked.

"Stay put, pard. I'm going to gather some camouflage to assist our getaway. If you guys spy anything that will give us some cover, bring it in." As was his custom, One-Zero disappeared, soundlessly.

"Okay, Dad, what's around here we can use?" Nicky Neill turned back to survey the river.

"There!" Dr. Carpenter pointed across the stream. "Something's hung up on the other side."

"Yeah, I see it. Good eyes! I'll fetch it." Nicky Neill kept to the shadows, lightly treading water toward the opposite bank. He submerged as much of himself as possible and worked his way beside the object. In short order, he was back with his father. A large piece of thatched roofing trailed after him, bobbing erratically in the current.

"Good work, son." Dr. Carpenter helped to secure their prize. "It'll be good to have a roof over our heads again, huh!"

"Nice one, Dad!"

Father and son waited beneath the bridge until One-Zero reappeared. He showed up without fanfare, his body all but obscured by a stack of vegetation that trailed from his shoulders to the ground.

"Ready to go with the flow?" he asked as he eased into the water beside his friends. "Nice roof!" he added. "Create your cover, boys."

"I'll go with Dad," Nicky Neill said.

"Right," One-Zero acknowledged. "Remember, stay close to the far side an' keep driftin' until you spot the big yellow tree. I stashed a boat under that tree. If our luck holds, Ploox should be curled up beneath it."

"So, we find the boat and Ploox and hightail it out of here, right?"

"That's the plan." One-Zero pulled more foliage over his head until he was invisible. "One more thing. Whatever you hear, whatever commotion breaks loose, don't leave your cover."

"We'll stay put," Nicky Neill promised.

"If the Lacandon see us, they might never stop chasing us. ¿Comprende?"

"Yeah. Comprendo."

"Okay, then, fellow fugitives, let's shove off!" One-Zero pushed away from the bank, launching his clump into the current. Nicky Neill and his father watched as the mass of debris tacked close to the opposite shore and disappeared around the bend in the river.

"Our turn, Dad. Here we go." Nicky Neill and Dr. Carpenter pushed off. The pull of the current, aided by furiously kicking feet, delivered them to the far side of the waterway by the time they negotiated the dogleg.

CHAPTER 68

When Nicky Neill and Dr. Carpenter and their island of floating debris rounded the curve, they spotted dark columns of smoke spiraling into the sky above the village. On the ground, billowing clouds of sooty gray fog fanned out in all directions. Above all of this, a strident rumble of conch shells and human voices resounded in the background. A hundred yards downstream a swarm of Lacandon was amassed in the river, filling and returning ceramic pots as fast as humanly possible. The containers were passed from one set of hands to the next, all the way back to the source of the blaze.

"Oh, my gosh, Dad! What have we done?"

"It may not be as bad as it appears, son." Dr. Carpenter's response was hushed and tentative.

The choking clouds of grit and smoke that drifted across the river added to the fugitives' cover. It did not take long for them to drift clear of the bedlam. Beyond the bucket brigade they faced open water.

Nicky Neill peered hard into the emerald distance, searching for a clue of One-Zero and the yellow tree. But there was no sign of either. Ten minutes more of floating with the current delivered them to another twist in the river. When they emerged from the latest curve, a wider, faster-moving body of water confronted them.

"Hey!" Dr. Carpenter's voice pierced the silence. "Look! On the right, up ahead!"

"What, Dad? What is it?" A withered palm frond that had shifted position across his face obstructed Nicky Neill's view. "I can't see a blasted thing."

"It's the yellow tree, son, the one we're looking for."

Nicky Neill pushed away from the island altogether and reemerged in the open water.

"You're right, Dad! That's got to be it! And that's one big wall of rock beside us."

Several hundred yards downstream a bright yellow sphere stood out like a sun ball floating upon the canopy. It was an extraordinary sight. An odd mountain of black stone paralleled the river's bank, just as One-Zero had described.

"I think it's a cortez tree. It's magnificent!"

"Yeah," Nicky Neill returned to his cover, "it's fit for a king."

Father and son guided their debris heap closer to the bank, but not too close. Nicky Neill pushed aside the urge to celebrate and focused on all that could go wrong. Ploox and Jorge could have been captured already. A platoon of Lacandon warriors could be lying in wait near the canoe, poised for an ambush. Even One-Zero might be a prisoner by now. It was not inconceivable that Jaguar Man had crossed into this world and was in charge of the search-and-destroy mission himself. Nicky Neill's spirits began to sink. He knew, from these weeks on the road, that the unexpected had a way of asserting itself. The beautiful yellow tree in the closing distance began losing its luster with each passing second.

CHAPTER 69

*T*he discarded segment of thatched roof bumped against the lush bank of the river and bobbed gently beside it. Seconds ebbed into minutes. An uneasy tension set in. Nicky Neill moved closer to his father. He had formed a plan and was ready to share it.

"Nick! Nick!" Two words clicked from somewhere in the forest above them.

"Huh?" Nicky Neill whispered to his father. "Did you hear that, Dad?"

"I think I heard something," he murmured. "I'm not sure."

"Nick!" This time there was no mistaking it.

"Yes!" Nicky Neill called back. "Who is it?"

"Me, pard! Get outta the water! Do it quietly."

"One-Zero! Yeah, we're coming!" Nicky Neill wrapped an arm around his father's shoulder. "You first, Dad. Stay low, move to the tree."

"Okay, son. Will do." Dr. Carpenter found a handhold and began to pull himself from the river. Nicky Neill steadied him from below.

When his father had cleared the bank and disappeared into the foliage, Nicky Neill followed after. He found his dad hunched down beneath an elephant leaf. One-Zero sat cross-legged beside him.

"You boys took your sweet time," he said. "Any sign that you were followed?"

"No, sir. Not that we could tell." Nicky Neill hesitated. "We brought the hammer down on the village, man. I...I don't feel good about that. All those people..."

"Hmm." One-Zero nodded in agreement. "I understand. Know this; it looks a lot worse than it really is. Bamboo makes for lousy fuel." He winked at Nicky Neill. "What's next, pard?"

"What's next? We find Ploox, jump in the boat, and get the heck out of here! Am I wrong?"

"Ah, right you are. All we need, then, is Ploox and the boat." One-Zero did not move.

"Okay then, we find the boat. Dad, we're looking for a boat somewhere close to this tree." Nicky Neill nodded toward the towering cortez.

"I understand, son, but as far as I can tell, there's no boat beneath the tree...or anywhere near it." Dr. Carpenter looked beyond their position and studied the bush.

"Oh, it's here, Dad. Trust me, it's right under our noses." Nicky Neill moved to the tree's enormous trunk and slowly circled it. There was no sign of a boat of any shape or size. He was about to complain that this was not the time or place for riddles when the notion struck him. He had to think like One-Zero...where would his friend hide a boat? How would he hide a boat? A knowing smile spread across Nicky Neill's contorted face. "You're a funny guy, One-Zero."

Nicky Neill moved away from the base of the tree and crept toward a darkened patch of forest. He stopped beside a fallen timber long rotted from exposure to termites and temperature.

"Ploox!" he hissed. "You better be ready to travel!" Nicky Neill took hold of a section of the decomposing remains and pulled. The wood disintegrated in his hands. He pushed hard against the clump of moldy debris and the entire mound collapsed at his feet. In the dim light, beneath a mess of compost, the hull of a boat revealed itself.

"I knew it!" In a near frenzy, Nicky Neill pushed aside the rubbish until he cleared a wide swath of canoe. "It's a dugout. It's upside down." With every ounce of strength he could muster, Nicky Neill attempted to turn the craft over, but it would not budge. "Dang! This thing weighs a ton!"

"C'mon, already!" a voice called out from beneath the boat. "Lemme give ya a hand."

With a great swooshing sound, the dugout rose up and then crashed down at Nicky Neill's feet. It was all he could do to get clear of the avalanche. In the process of backpedaling, he tripped and tumbled onto the jungle floor.

A great cloud of dust exploded, rising into the air above the canoe. From the choking mist a figure emerged, offering an outstretched hand.

"Yuh don't have to bow to the king no more, Nicky Neill! I quit that gig this mornin'."

"Ploox!" Nicky Neill sprang to his feet. "Ploox! Ploox! Man, it's good to see you!" They hugged, like family long lost. "Hey!" he exclaimed, stepping back from his friend. "Where's your clothes?"

Ploox stood before him sporting nothing more than a well-soiled tunic and a bundle tucked under his arm. He was still wearing his medallion around his neck.

"To tell yuh the truth, Ah'm lucky to be here at all...least I got this nasty dress!"

CHAPTER 70

"George Plucowski!" Dr. Carpenter stepped into a narrow shaft of sunlight and peered incredulously at the bedraggled figure beside his son.

"Yup, it's me all right, Doc. An' Ah'm mighty glad ta see ya!" Ploox bound through the vegetation and bear-hugged Nicky Neill's dad, lifting him off the ground in the process. "Yuh look like yuh been through yer own adventure, Perfessor! But yer alive an' we got ya now!"

The long-anticipated reunion was set to pick up steam, but One-Zero cut it short.

"Fellas, I know you all got a lot to talk about, but that'll have to wait a bit...we ain't in the clear just yet."

"You're right." Nicky Neill returned to the dugout. "It will take all of us to get this log to the river."

Sliding the canoe through the undergrowth was no easy task. When they reached the riverbank, the procession stopped. All ears were in the wind; every set of eyes scanned the stream and the surrounding forest.

"All clear," Nicky Neill whispered, "for the moment."

"Appears so," One-Zero agreed. "Let's launch."

The big dugout eased into the water with hardly a splash.

"Okay," One-Zero announced, "let's board. An' just to be on the side of caution, I'd like you guys to lie down. Once we're clear of Lacandon territory, you can pop up and help me paddle. Fair enough?"

"Yuh want it to look like yur on yer own, right?" Ploox winked at One-Zero as he stepped into the dugout.

"Ploox, you may not be a king any longer, but you still think like one!" One-Zero laughed. When everyone was on board, he pushed off the bank. The canoe slipped easily into the current. For the first few minutes, the only sound to be heard was the gentle splash of One-Zero's paddle rhythmically churning the water.

"Hey, Ploox!" It was all Nicky Neill could do to hold his voice to a near whisper. "What happened this morning, with the escape and all?"

"Oh, man! Yuh wouldn't believe it! Know why Ah ain't got muh outfit on?"

"Because Hector told you to leave it behind?"

"Uh-huh, no, sir! Hector never told me nothin' like that. Maybe cuz he didn't have the chance to."

"What do you mean?"

"Ah wuz jus' climbin' on to that clothesline rig to slide outta the palace when the bomb goes off..."

"What! That thing wasn't supposed to explode until after you were out of there!"

"Yeah, well, someone shoulda told the bomb that! Anyhow, it blew me right offa that rope! When Ah hit the ground, Ah wuz on fire. Ah rolled aroun' in the dirt till Ah quit burnin', then Ah stripped down to muh undies and waited fer Hector to show up."

"You were on fire, Ploox? Like, flames and all?" The grin evaporated from Nicky Neill's face.

"Hector rolled muh clothes up in a bundle, give me this here tunic, an' then we hightailed it to the river!"

"Didn't anybody try to stop you? You are the king, after all."

"Hah! Hector threw a blanket over me; nobody could see who Ah wuz. We just ran all the way, right through the village an' all them people. Ah swear, they musta thought the world wuz endin'...folks wuz in a panic!"

"Oh, man!" Nicky Neill rolled to his side and looked into Ploox's face. "The place looked like a war zone when we floated by."

"Yeah. Hee-yuk! That palace, it split apart an' the biggest danged fireball ever shot out straight up in the air...then a bunch o' giant black clouds followed after." Ploox sighed and exhaled. "Nicky Neill, it wuz like a volcano got born right underneath me! Ah think Ah'm lucky ta be alive, ta tell yuh the truth."

"Oh, man...I couldn't agree more. In fact, it's pretty much a miracle that we're all here, you know?"

"Boys," Dr. Carpenter joined the conversation, "when we get to a safer place, I'd really like to hear a full account of your odyssey..."

"Oh, m'gosh, Dr. C! You'll need a coupla days fer this story!"

"That story is not quite finished yet," One-Zero said. "We got company."

"What's happening?" Nicky Neill fought the urge to rise up and look behind them.

"There's two canoes of warriors on our tail. I reckon they're not but one of several teams out sweepin' the area. Whatever the case, they're in hot pursuit."

"Whut can we do?" Ploox asked.

"Nothin' yet." One-Zero's face lit up. "It'll be a cold day in the tropics when anybody catches me from behind in a canoe race. Besides, they're still out of bow range, and Jorge's less

"Our heroes make a speedy getaway"

than a quarter mile downriver. You fellas just keep layin' low an' try not to let the G-force compress your spines!"

"Hee-yuk!" Ploox squealed. "Ah'm buckled in an' ready ta fly! Bring it on!"

CHAPTER 71

*T*he canoe shot forward. One-Zero's breathing became labored and rhythmic. The sound of the paddle striking the water resonated like machinegun fire exploding beside the dugout.

"There!" One-Zero grunted. "The elbow turn: Jorge will be waitin' not far from that bend. Get ready, boys!"

"Ready for what?" Nicky Neill raised his head.

"You fellas will bail out and scamper into the bush. Jorge will find you. He's got the horses and his donkey, too, I imagine. He knows a shortcut to Palenque. By tonight you guys will have full bellies and clean clothes. And," he added, "you'll be surrounded by familiar faces."

"What about you?" Nicky Neill demanded. "We're not leaving you!"

"Oh, yes you are, Nick. This is how you found me! Besides, I have to lead these warriors on a goose chase, savvy?"

"Yes, sir. I do. But I don't like it." Nicky Neill looked into his friend's eyes.

"Likin' it don't matter, little brother. It's what you do that matters. Get ready now!" One-Zero guided the dugout alongside the river's bank. He found a handhold and the boat came to a momentary halt. "Out, boys! Out! Be quick about it!"

Ploox shot from the canoe to the densely forested bank and turned toward Dr. Carpenter. "Come on, Doc! Take muh hand!"

Dr. Carpenter reached for Ploox and jumped. When he found his footing on the embankment, he spun about to face the boat. "Sir," he looked to One-Zero, "I have no idea who you are, but I will be thankful to you for as long as I live."

One-Zero grinned in response. "Live a long time, Professor. It's these boys you should be thankin'."

"Come on, Dr. C! Foller me!" Ploox pulled Dr. Carpenter into the underbrush. Seconds later, he reappeared. "Hey, One-Zero! Thanks fer ever'thang, yuh know? An' pass that on ta Helen fer me, if ya will!"

"Will do, King. Till we meet again!"

"Yep, till then, big guy!" Ploox disappeared into the vegetation a final time.

"So." Nicky Neill stood up in the dugout. He stared hard at his friend. "I don't know how to thank you."

"Sure you do, pard. Live a good life. And never forget what you did here. Now, go, Nick! Make the world a better place."

Nicky Neill jumped to the shoreline and turned for one last look at the most incredible human being he had ever met.

"Tell Helen..."

"Yep, I'll tell her. And by the way, this is for you." One-Zero dug into his mystery pouch and withdrew an object. "Catch!"

Nicky Neill's hands shot out and captured a strangely textured, heavy object. "What?" he sputtered.

"From the ball game, pard. Don't hurt yourself! Oh, pass this on to Ploox!" A bundle flew over Nicky Neill's head. "It'll have to do until he gets some proper trousers." One-Zero jabbed the paddle into the river's bank and pushed hard. The canoe lurched into the stream and immediately picked up speed. In a matter of seconds, he vanished.

"C'mon, Nicky Neill!" Ploox called out. "We're waitin' on yuh!"

Nicky Neill plowed into the forest toward the sound of his friend's voice. In the distance he could hear Mayan voices. Their cries blended together until they resembled the hum of angry hornets, searching the air for whatever had disturbed their nest. Before long, their buzzing faded and the river fell silent.

"Ploox! Dad!" Nicky Neill called out. "I'm coming!"

CHAPTER 72

"Who is Jorge, son?" Dr. Carpenter posed the question over his shoulder. He was working hard to keep up with Ploox.

"He's a good friend, Dad. A real friend, like One-Zero." As he spoke, Nicky Neill scanned the jungle around them. There was no safety in the bush, warriors or not.

"Yuh ain't never met a kid like Jorge, Doc." Ploox laughed out loud. "Somethin' new ever' day!"

"¡Oye, Rey! You remember *mi lema!*" an exuberant voice called out in the near distance.

"Jorge!" Ploox crowed. "Whut took yuh so long!"

An oddly camouflaged figure popped into view ahead of them.

"Aminuevos! Ees so good to see you...so very, very good!" Jorge darted forward, as did Ploox. They crashed together and toppled to the forest floor.

"Ee-yuk!" Ploox chortled.

"Dad." Nicky Neill took his father's arm and guided him beside the writhing figures at their feet. "This is Jorge. At least, it sounds like him!"

Jorge sprang to his feet and dusted himself off. With that, a hand shot upward and removed a sombrero from his head. All in the same motion, he bowed low toward Dr. Carpenter.

"Jorge Campo at your service, señor."

Dr. Carpenter held out his hand. Jorge shook it warmly. "It's a pleasure, Jorge. I look forward to getting to know you."

"*Sí, profe,* me too." Jorge smiled and drank in the vision of his friends. "We weel celebrate later, my freens. Right now, we got to fly. Thees woods, she ees alive weeth warriors!" Jorge paused and looked Ploox over. "Ploox! *¿Dónde está la ropa real?*"

"Oh!" Ploox blushed. "They burnt right off o' me in the explosion! Ah'm lucky to have this here dress."

"Eeksplosion?" Jorge stared harder at his friend.

"We'll catch up on everything later, guys. By the way, Ploox, One-Zero wanted you to have these." Nicky Neill passed the bundle to his pal. "Here."

Ploox grasped the object and unrolled it.

"Dang! Is this another dress?"

"No, ees a warrior's breeches, amigo. An' you gotta git een theem pronto, 'cause we hafta move. ¡Rápido!"

Ploox wriggled into the garment and tied off the waist string. He smiled sheepishly at his companions. The skirt fell just above his knees.

"Well," he sighed, "beats traipsin' aroun' in a nightgown! Let's go! Ah don't wanna meet them soldiers again."

"Thees way!" Jorge spun about and set off through the jungle. Three figures shadowed him. They hiked in silence for a good fifteen minutes until Jorge stopped and knelt low to the earth.

"Whut is it, Jorge?" Ploox crowded beside him and dropped to a knee. "Didja hear somethin'?"

"Mira, Ploox." Jorge pointed off to one side. "What do you see?"

Ploox followed the line of his friend's finger. For a moment, he appeared confused. Then a knowing smile spread across his face.

"Legs!" He chuckled. "Horses' legs and a donkey's tail! Hot diggity, no more walkin' fer this crew!"

Jorge popped to his feet. "Come, compadres! Your old freens are waiting."

Ten yards ahead, Bandit, Pancho, and Jorge's dingy burro waited.

"They look fit," Nicky Neill said.

"Yeah," Ploox agreed. Pancho pressed his muzzle into the boy's chest. "Ah think they're glad ta see us, Nicky Neill. Lookit!"

"Sí, thees are workeeng ponies...an' they are ready to work! C'mon, we mount up." Jorge swung onto his burro and goaded him into the jungle. "Queekly, muchachos! The Lacandon *guerreros* don't geeve up so eesily." In the blink of an eye, the forest swallowed them up.

"Me and Dad on Bandit." Nicky Neill swung into the saddle. "Ploox, can you give Dad a hand?"

"You betcha! Give me yer foot, Doc." Ploox hoisted Dr. Carpenter into position. "You good, sir?"

"Yes, George. Thanks, I'm fine. You better mount up yourself. Your friend has already disappeared."

"Not to worry, Dr. C. These horses already know where we're goin'!" Ploox guided a foot into a dangling stirrup. "This is gonna be weird!" he murmured, settling into the saddle. "Let's git! Ah'll foller you guys."

CHAPTER 73

*T*hey rode in silence. Nicky Neill was certain they were
not the only people in the jungle. The Lacandon warriors knew these woods like he knew the backyards in his
neighborhood at home. Fear of ambush was a real concern.
They were not in the clear yet, far from it.

At one point, they moved through a natural clearing and
Nicky Neill noticed that the sun was directly overhead. That
meant they had been on the move at least five hours since
their escape from the lost world. Exhaustion had not struck
him yet, but he knew it was coming.

Jorge raised an arm. The caravan came to a halt. Nicky
Neill discovered it took all the strength he could muster to rein
in his mount.

"Whoa! Whut is it?" Ploox leaned across his saddle.

"Ees no problem, jus' a question I haf' to ask you. Okay?"

"Shoot, Jorge." Nicky Neill guided Bandit closer to the little burro.

"*Bueno.* We haf a choice heer. We can go straight ahead
through thee forest an' reach Palenque een maybe three, four
more hours. Or," he hesitated and looked Dr. Carpenter over
closely, "we can go over thees heel, through very theek jongle
on thee other side, an' look for a peasant trail I heard about.
Eef we can find eet then we gonna follow eet to town."

"Whut's the advantage of the trail, Jorge?"

"Well, from thees trail ees only an hour or so to town."

"Uh-huh." Ploox shrugged. "But whut's the catch?"

"Ah, sí, thee catch. Well, ees a rough ride. Thees heel, she
ees ugly. *Muy fea.*" Jorge's free hand planed upward with only
a slight angle. "Almos' straight up an' thee other side, pretty
much straight down...ees hard on thee animals an' very hard

on thee riders." He hesitated, looking directly to Nicky Neill
and his passenger. "Easy to, uh, how you say, fall...fall off thee
horse. ¿Comprenden?"

Nicky Neill twisted in the saddle. "Dad?"

"The shortest route is not always the best course." Dr. Carpenter's voice was weak, hardly more than a whisper. "But in
this case, it's the best call. I think I can manage another
hour...maybe. More than that...not so sure. Let's give it a shot,
men."

A pained expression spread over Jorge's face. "I am not jus'
worried 'bout Papá," he said.

"Know whut?" Ploox slid from Pancho's saddle and hit the
ground, beaming with confidence. "Ah got it. Nicky Neill, you
mount up on Pancho. An' you, Doc, you climb inta that saddle, see? Ah'll ride behind Dr. C an' keep him steady. Meantime, fergit them reins, Nicky Neill. You jus' hang on ta that
saddle horn an' try ta stay awake! C'mon, let's trade places!"

Ploox had to lower Nicky Neill to the ground. Afterward,
he guided his friend's foot into the stirrup and lifted him to
the saddle. Then, with all the grace his skirt would allow,
Ploox launched himself onto Bandit's haunches and secured
the reins, encircling Dr. Carpenter with both arms.

"There!" he announced. "Let's tackle that hill."

CHAPTER 74

*T*he riders continued on another hundred yards when a wall of jungle rose up before them like a rampart. Their progress came to an abrupt halt. It had not become visible until they confronted it, but now the rugged nature of their choice made itself apparent.

"Man!" Ploox marveled. "We could go 'round this cloud-kisser, huh?"

"Sí, an' as you can eemagine now, goin' 'round ees not a bad choice."

"Yup, that's purty clear all right...this hill don't go nowhere but up." Ploox rocked back on Bandit's haunches and followed the contour of the slope as far as his neck would allow. "But then, where's the fun in that?"

"Ploox." Jorge pulled his furry mount closer to the former king. "You see what I see, amigo?"

"Uh-huh, Ah see it. Exhaustion, plain and simple. I reckon Nicky Neill's been pushin' the envelope o' days, an' Dr. C, well, Ah cain't hardly imagine whut he's done been through..." Ploox studied Jorge's sympathetic gaze. "That's why we gotta git 'em ta Palenque as fast as we can. Whuttya think, amigo?"

"Sí, I agree. Thee pain, she ees deeper over thee mountain, but she don't last so long thees way." Jorge twisted around and surveyed their challenge. "What am I theenkin', man?" He slid from his burro and untied the makeshift rope halter. Without a word, he secured one end of the rigging to Nicky Neill's saddle. With some effort, Jorge made his way to Pancho's rump and tied the other end off on the saddle horn. "Okay! You keep Papá een thee saddle an' I do thee same for Neek."

"Yer a good man, Jorge!" Ploox smiled. "We better git. You lead the way."

From the outset the horses were compelled to lunge. The initial launch sent Nicky Neill's head crashing into Jorge's face. He shook off the sting and swayed to the right with each successive assault.

On Nicky Neill's part, the first explosion to the back of the head was perceived as a blow from a Mayan war club, but he was determined to keep moving. The heaviness in his head soon transformed into an ongoing hallucinatory state as he struggled to maintain consciousness.

The ascent up the mountain was more than a vertical challenge; the riders were still immersed in rain forest. Everything in the jungle contested their progress. Worst of all was the possibility that Bandit or Pancho would lose their footing and topple backward, head over hooves, into a fall that could not be arrested. Nicky Neill and Dr. Carpenter remained silent except to cry out or moan when the agony became unbearable. Ploox and Jorge managed their tasks in heroic fashion, keeping their co-riders in the saddle, urging the horses on when they wanted to stop.

The climb seemed to go on forever. Time peeled away, measured only by pain and brief intervals between the last torment and the next. Then, abruptly, the riders breached the summit. What confronted them now was the descent, an experience that promised nothing less than a mirrored version of their fight to the top.

CHAPTER 75

*A*t the mountain's peak an expansive view of the turquoise sky overhead stretched away in every direction.

"Looks like a fire scorched this here hilltop, once't upon a time, huh?" Ploox said.

"*Sí,*" Jorge sighed. "*Aquí la montaña está calva.*"

"Say whut?" Ploox turned toward his friend.

"Sorry, Ploox. I say heer thee mountain she ees bald. An' I am thankful, no? 'Cos we get a leetle break from thee jongle an' also, we get a peek at thee sky...*ai qué maravilla!*"

"Yup, yer sure right 'bout that...it is a wonder. Them clouds're gigantic, too. Lookit yonder. That'n looks like a dadblamed pyramid!"

"Huh?" Nicky Neill struggled through squinted eyes to scan the vista overhead. "Yeah! Yeah!" he began to shout. "That's the main pyramid! That's the one! Come on, we can't stay here!" A fierce clap of thunder erupted above them, shaking the mountain itself. "The drums! The war drums! They're coming after us, I'm telling you!" Nicky Neill was yelling at the top of his lungs. Another burst of thunder shook the earth, followed by an explosion of rain. "It's them!" he cried out. "It's the warriors, they're out! They'll be all over us! Run! Run, guys! Run like you never ran before!" Nicky Neill lowered his head and began flailing his arms as if he were racing at breakneck speed.

"Dang!" Ploox gasped. "C'mon, Jorge, Nicky Neill's hallucinatin' somethin' awful. Let's git!" He jabbed his heels into Bandit's flanks. "Giddy up, Bandit! Let's git offa this mountain!"

Bandit led the way, crashing into the forest with a burst of speed that astonished his rider. Pancho fell in close behind, leaving Jorge's little burro alone on the hilltop amidst the lightning and the pelting rain.

The journey down was similar to the climb up, only in reverse. Both riders let loose of their reins. With one hand they clutched lightly at the saddle horn; the other arm encircled their respective passenger.

Although the canopy provided some protection from the rain, it was hardly enough. Once-dry saddles were converted to slippery launch pads. For the first time since they began their escape on horseback, riders and passengers alike were subjected to relentless plunges to the forest floor. Agonizing is too gentle a word to describe the trip down the mountain.

Ploox and Jorge were not to be deterred. Again and again they regrouped and remounted after each spill. Nicky Neill and Dr. Carpenter were beyond delirious. They miraculously emerged from each ejection with no broken bones or gaping wounds. The same was true for Jorge and Ploox. They all blurred into soggy, filthy versions of human beings. Or, as Ploox began calling themselves, "draggle people."

"¡Allí, Ploox!" Jorge called out, pointing into the mist and fog.

"Yeah? Whut is it? Tell me it ain't a cliff or a jaguar!"

"¡No, no amigo! Ees not thees...ees thee bottom, I theenk. Mira, you see eet?"

Ploox swiped his brow with a muddied hand. "Dang!" Releasing his grip on the saddle horn, he ducked his forehead beneath his tunic and cleared his eyes of enough debris and moisture to allow a better view of the landscape ahead. "Oh, m'gosh! Ah think yer right. We're comin' off the mountain!"

The horses reached level ground and momentarily stalled out.

"Whut now, Jorge?"

"We find thee trail, mi rey, an' then we ride home. No?"

"Yup!" Ploox responded. "We ride home."

CHAPTER 76

J orge took the lead at the mountain's base. He had a good idea which way to go. Nicky Neill was no longer conscious. When they reached level ground, he had collapsed backward into Jorge's embrace, dead to the world. The rain continued to fall as if it would rain forever. No one spoke; no one had the energy to do much more than breathe.

As they wound their way through thick jungle, Jorge found himself lured into an expanding daydream. In his reverie he, along with his companions, stood before the gate of his hotel. He pulled incessantly upon the bell string, reveling in the familiar sound it made. The bell led to Mamá and her warm kitchen. As he waited outside the gate, he detected a subtle change in Pancho's stride and an even more delicate shift in the horse's direction.

"¿Qué?" He bolted upright in spite of the weight of his passenger. "¿Dónde estamos?"

"Whut's up, Jorge?" Ploox called out.

"There! Thee trail...I see eet. Pancho, he find eet all by heemself! *Gracias a Diós*, Ploox! We be home soon, my freen."

"Great job, Jorge! Great job! An' just in time, too. Ah've had to pee somethin' fierce fer the longest while!"

The horses plodded on for the next half hour. They anticipated a warm stall and a mound of dry hay. They knew home was close by.

Unexpectedly, the forest gave way to a vast pasture. In the distance, the town of Palenque wavered in the steady downpour like some imagined oasis.

"Well," Ploox sighed, guiding Bandit closer to Pancho. "Yuh got a doctor in town?"

"No, but we weel find somebody."

"Yeah, Ah know yuh will...yuh always come through." Ploox licked at the rain that ran across his face. "Oh, one more question."

"*Si, amigo.* Ask away."

"Ah know this is gonna sound kinda dumb, but yuh reckon muh laundry is done by now? I gotta git outta this skirt!"

For the first time in a long while, Jorge laughed. It began as a giggle, but it soon expanded to a gut-busting, sidesplitting roar. And it was contagious. Together, the riders laughed all the way into town.

CHAPTER 77

Somewhere, on a distant peninsula of consciousness, Nicky Neill detected voices. At first, he made no real effort to understand them. Their pleasant droning offered a calming background effect on the edge of his latest dream. In his dream world, there were no fierce warriors in pursuit, no small vipers lying in ambush. No Jaguar Man. But his attention was gradually drawn to the voices. There was something familiar in the way they rang in his ears. His mind struggled to identify them. In a spasm of delirious expectation, his eyes popped open.

"Mom! Mom! Is that you?" Nicky Neill rolled his head toward the source of the words. His eyes were encrusted with sleep and his vision was blurred. But his ears worked fine.

"Nicholas! It's me, dear!" His mother rushed to his side. "Easy does it, son. I'm here, and so are Grandma and Phin and Ellen. Everything is okay; you're safe."

"What about Dad? And Ploox? And Jorge? Where are they?"

"They're all here, dear. Everyone is here. And everyone is going to be fine." She turned away for an instant and called out over her shoulder. "Dr. Geffers! Dr. Geffers! Nicky Neill is awake! Come quickly!" Then she returned to her boy and hovered above him, stroking his head as if he were a helpless infant.

"Am I home, Mom? What's going on?"

"Now, now, son," Dr. Geffers cautioned. "It's understandable you're disoriented. You're still in Mexico. Since you and your father weren't in any shape to come to us, we came to you." Dr. Geffers cleared his throat and pulled a chair up beside Nicky Neill's bed. "Relax for a moment, if you will. And don't speak. I want to look you over." Dr. Geffers proceeded to conduct his ritual. "Well," he sighed, putting his instruments away, "for the time being there's no cause for alarm. Of course, there'll be extensive testing to perform when we get back home. But you and your father are at no apparent risk at the moment."

"Oh, my gosh!" Nicky Neill bolted upright in his bed. "Where is Dad? Have you checked Ploox out, too? Have you met Jorge? Did you..."

"Easy, son. Your dad is still resting. In fact, he's sedated in the next room."

"What's wrong with him, sir?" Nicky Neill looked directly into Dr. Geffers' eyes. With some effort, he steadied himself on one elbow.

"Well, Nick," Dr. Geffers glanced at Mrs. Carpenter, who nodded approvingly, "considering the conditions of his captivity he's not faring too badly. He, um, has some parasites and I'm treating him for those. He's on antibiotics as well and that will help a lot. He was extremely dehydrated when he arrived here and, uh, he was covered in some nasty insect bites. Now, all that being said," he leaned closer and clasped Nicky Neill's hand, "your dad's going to recover from all of this. A complete recovery, you understand?"

"Yes, sir. I do. Thanks. That's what I needed to hear." Nicky Neill eased back onto his pillow only to spring upright again. "How did you guys know where we were? How did you find us?"

Mrs. Carpenter moved beside Dr. Geffers. Her smile brought tears to Nicky Neill's eyes.

"A Dr. Xama called us three days ago. She told us you and George would be bringing Dad to Palenque and that we should come down as quickly as possible. We contacted Dr. Geffers. He called Dr. Benner at the college and the president secured a plane for us. We all flew down together, direct to Palenque."

"What?" Nicky Neill was astounded.

"That's not all, Nicky Neill!" Phin crowded in between Dr. Geffers and his mother. "Get this! There's no airport here, so you know what? We landed on the road and then we taxied right into town! Right into town, man!"

"You're kidding!" Nicky Neill sat up in bed and opened his arms for his brother to fall into. "I'm so glad to see you, buddy! Hey! Where's Ellen?"

"Oh, she's with Margarita and Rosa. They're teaching her how to make tortillas!" Phin pulled away from his brother's embrace and stared hard at the thin, sunburned face looking back at him. "You did it, Nicky Neill...you really did it!" Tears welled up and began to spill from Phin's fast-blinking eyes. "I knew you'd do it. I knew you wouldn't let us be orphans!"

Phin laughed and cried and laughed some more. Then Grandma crowded into their tight little circle. Everyone was crying. Everyone was laughing.

Nicky Neill caught his breath at last and glanced nervously around the room. "Say, where's Ploox, anyway?"

"Oh," his mother replied, dabbing at her tear-stained cheeks, "where do you think?"

"Right," Nicky Neill acknowledged. "Making tortillas in the kitchen!"

Before long, Mrs. Carpenter encouraged everyone to allow Nicky Neill some time to get dressed. When the room was cleared, she stood before him, smiling down at her son. There was a wistful look in her eyes Nicky Neill had never seen before.

"Mom, are you mad at me?" Before she could answer, he continued. "I ran away from home. I should never have done that. I can only imagine the pain I put you through. I'm sorry, Mom. I'm so sorry...I just didn't want anything to happen to you, too."

"Sssh. It's all done now," she whispered, moving closer to the bed. "It's done and I understand. Phin told me everything." She fell silent and studied her boy. "It's a miracle, Nicky Neill. Your father is safe and will be himself again soon.

And George Plucowski is not the same boy who left with you. And you..." Her words trailed off. Tears filled her eyes again.

"Please, Mom. Don't cry. You seem sad. We're all going to be okay, just like Dr. Geffers said."

"Yes, yes, I know. It's not that, honey. It's just...yesterday you were my little boy...and now, you're not that same boy anymore. I didn't expect you to grow up so fast."

She bent low and cradled his head in her arms. There was nothing more to say. Not at that moment.

CHAPTER 78

*T*he Carpenter family, along with Dr. Geffers and the college pilot who flew them all down to Mexico, remained at the Hotel Maya in Palenque for a full week.

Dr. Carpenter's health was the initial concern. As soon as the four travelers reached the hotel that rainy afternoon, Dr. Geffers began his examinations, first on the professor and then Nicky Neill, followed by Ploox and Jorge. All of his patients were dehydrated. Nicky Neill's feet were lacerated and evidence of infection was visible to the naked eye. Dr. Carpenter's case was more severe. He was infested with parasites, an upper respiratory infection that made breathing difficult, and he was covered with nasty, oozing insect bites that resembled bullet holes. The pain from the bites was agonizing. Dr. Geffers carried antibiotics in his medical bag and these he administered to both men. The parasites and the bites, however, were more troubling. He wrestled with the issue of which medication to use that would be more toxic to the parasite than to the patient. The following morning, to help clarify his choices, he talked the issue over with Grandma Carpenter. Quite unintentionally, Jorge overheard the exchange between the two.

"*Perdón, Doctór,*" he interjected. "I overheer your conversation with Abuelita an' I theenk I can help you."

"Jorge, I would be more than happy to hear your thoughts. I've never seen such bites in my entire career. Do you have experience with this sort of wound?"

"*Sí, señor,* I have seen thees theeng before. But I have no experience myself. However, I know somebody who can help."

Jorge left the hotel immediately. He was gone for several hours. When he returned he was accompanied by his own grandmother and another woman; someone the likes of whom most of the newcomers had never seen before.

Everyone was in the dining area listening to the radio when Jorge arrived. Mrs. Carpenter sat between Phin and Ellen on the leather bench. Dr. Carpenter was slouched in a hammock chair suspended from a broad beam in the high ceiling. Ploox and Nicky Neill were on hand as well, pleasantly crowded onto a sofa with Margarita and Rosa. Grandma was in the kitchen with Señora Campo and Constancia. They came out as soon as Jorge and his guests appeared. Dr. Geffers was studying a medical journal, sipping coffee at the end of a hand-carved table. He looked up expectantly at the new arrivals.

"*Doctór*," Jorge announced. "I am back." He flashed a broad smile at the roomful of family and friends, then turned to introduce his companions. "For those of you who don't know, thees ees my own *abuela*, thee mother of my mother. She ees Doña Nikté. An' her freen ees Doña Ts'aakik. Maybe," Jorge added innocently, "you can see thees ladies are pure Maya?"

For a moment, no one moved or even spoke. Señora Campo smiled warmly at her mother and nodded respectfully at her companion. Constancia, along with Margarita and Rosa, lowered their heads in deference. Everyone else in the dining room continued to study the new arrivals.

"So," Jorge continued, "Doña Ts'aakik ees a *curandera* and my abuela ees heer to help an' to translate. Doña Ts'aakik," he paused to look over the faces of his guests, "she don't speak Spanish so well."

Dr. Geffers rose from his chair and approached the tiny figures framed in the archway that separated the plaza from the dining area. As he moved toward them, Señora Campo turned off the radio.

"*Buenos días, señoras.*" The doctor addressed the women in his best Spanish. When he stood before them, he bowed low and uttered the final expression in his Spanish lexicon. "*¡Bienvenidos!*"

Jorge's grandmother giggled and nodded humbly at Dr. Geffers. Doña Ts'aakik offered no such response. Instead, she looked the stranger over closely. At last, she turned to her companion and barked out a string of sounds and syllables that few of the guests had ever heard before. Dr. Carpenter separated from his chair and crossed the room, stopping alongside Dr. Geffers. He acknowledged the two women by addressing them in their own tongue. A smile creased Doña Ts'aakik's face. She placed a large satchel on the floor and pulled a chair up, motioning for Dr. Carpenter to take a seat. Thus began the work of the curandera.

CHAPTER 79

The poultices Doña Ts'aakik prepared and applied to Nicky Neill's feet and Dr. Carpenter's bites had an almost immediate healing effect. The compound she created for Dr. Carpenter's parasite affliction, however, became a topic for endless discussion. Her concoction took the form of a tea that was to be consumed three times daily for two days. Her remedy was noteworthy, initially, because of its odor. The smell of it wafting from the kitchen was so offensive that everyone save the two Mayan women and Dr. Carpenter fled the area. The secondary reaction to the brew was more pleasing. By the following morning Dr. Carpenter showed evidence of an astonishing recuperation. His vitality returned and he rejoined the family as the husband and father they had all so long anticipated. The reunion was complete: the Carpenter family was intact once again.

The remainder of the Oklahoman's days in Palenque passed quickly.

Ploox and Margarita became known as the invisible couple. No one, not even Jorge, knew where they went for hours on end. Ploox did manage to summon up the courage to speak to his parents on the only public telephone in town. The result of that conversation remained private, but Ploox did confide to Nicky Neill that it wasn't as disastrous as he had feared.

Nicky Neill split his time between his family, Rosa, and Jorge. He also insisted on working half days at the restaurant as a means of repaying the Campo family's generosity. His Spanish improved significantly as a result.

Dr. Carpenter passed some of his free time secluded in Jorge's office engaged in the writing process. It proved to be the most difficult undertaking of his career. He wrestled daily with the urge to tell all, while at the same time doing everything he could to protect the inhabitants of the lost world within the mountain. While he knew he had to account for his disappearance to the college, he also felt a genuine responsibility to the Lacandon. It was a heavy burden, one that he took very seriously.

Dr. Geffers left each morning with Doña Nikté and spent the remainder of the day in study with Doña Ts'aakik at her farm on the jungle's edge. By the time the hour of their departure arrived, the doctor had filled three legal pads with detailed drawings of plants, herbs, and insects.

The primary shared activity, the ritual that followed supper each evening, came to be known as The Telling.

After the dishes had been washed and put away, Jorge made a small fire in the *chimenea* situated in the corner of the *comedor* near the kitchen. While he tended to the blaze, the guests drew up an assortment of chairs and couches and organized them in a semicircle around the fireplace. Two chairs were strategically placed side by side, at the front of the arrangement, for Ploox and Nicky Neill. Grandma Carpenter

"Dr. Geffers receives some old world knowledge"

and Constancia prepared hot cocoa while the theater was under construction. When everyone was comfortably seated, Nicky Neill and Ploox related their stories of life on the road in search of a missing father. The Telling occurred each of the six nights the Oklahomans spent at the Hotel Maya. Jorge provided a simultaneous translation to the non-English-speaking members of the audience.

Like Dr. Carpenter, Ploox and Nicky Neill were careful when it came to talking about the Lacandon. As for Nicky Neill and Dr. Carpenter's perils in the lost world, there was no mention at all. Nicky Neill contained that entire account to a contrived version of events that told about a secretive Mayan clan who occupied an ancient ceremonial center in an unexplored region of the jungle. Dr. Carpenter took note of his son's version of the story. He also acknowledged that the boy who was no longer a boy had the capacity to suppress key facts in masterful fashion, a realization that caused him no end of speculation.

CHAPTER 80

*E*verything ends. The Oklahomans' stay at the Hotel Maya, their life in Palenque, the travelers' recuperative timeline, all converged on the sixth day of their reunion. Ploox and Nicky Neill were reluctant to think about the end of their shared adventure, their life on the road, the certainty of uncertainty. And they loathed the thought of leaving behind the Campo family and the magical life in the Hotel Maya, not to mention two young Mexican girls. Yet they ached for their old lives in Waterville, their old friends and the new possibilities that awaited them.

And so it came to be that on day six every word, every gesture, and every action carried tremendous significance. The day passed slowly and quickly at the same time. The final Telling stretched late into the evening. When the fire burned out, all of the guests and the Campo family retired to their quarters and the lights flickered off in the hotel.

Nicky Neill's head fell back on his pillow, but there was no sleep in his immediate future. His mind raced out of control, haphazardly spinning out faces and memories and scenes and smells and tastes of the past five weeks. He was staggered by the parade of images and individuals that looped before his mind's eye. Unexpectedly, he began to weep. He snapped upright and threw his legs over the side of the bed. He continued to cry. Plastering his hands over his eyes did nothing to stem the outpouring. He eventually began to laugh...at himself, at the ways of the world, but most of all at the joy of life and the promise of another day. At that instant, he heard Helen's voice.

"Huh?" He raised his head and strained to confirm what he thought he had heard.

"Nicholas!" Helen's voice called out his name.

Now he was certain it was her. He had not detected her voice with his ears. She was speaking to him in another way, like she had done once before.

"I'm coming, Helen! I'm coming!" He felt for his pants on the chair beside the bed and pulled them on. With all the stealth he could muster, he tiptoed to the door, twisted the door handle without a sound, and slipped into the open walkway beyond.

"Over here!" Helen's actual voice echoed from the shadows beyond the Campos' living quarters. "By the clotheslines!"

Nicky Neill gently closed the door behind him. It was just as dark outside as the interior of his room. He lingered for a few seconds, absorbing the night before he set off down the balcony toward the stairwell.

He moved like a shadow between the buildings and passed into the yard where Señora Campo dried her laundry. Along the far wall a cluster of chairs bordered the concrete table where Margarita and Constancia folded sheets. Helen would be there, waiting.

"Nicholas," she called out to him. "Thank you for coming."

He kissed the air beside her cheek, but she pulled him close and hugged him. "Are you okay?" he asked. "Is One-Zero all right?"

"Yes, we are both fine." She released him and eased into a nearby chair. "Sit," she said. "I've come to say good-bye."

"Yes, ma'am. I'm really glad to see you."

For a long moment, Helen was quiet.

"You know," she whispered, "this world was once barren rock."

"Ma'am?"

"Now it is a jewel. Knowingly or unknowingly, people seek to steal the jewel and replace it with a stone." Again, she fell silent. "There are two kinds of people in this world, Nicholas," she continued. "There are those who wish only to admire the jewel and there are those who wish to own it. This is the great paradox of human nature. Do you understand?"

"I...I'm...not sure, Helen."

"You want to know who One-Zero and I are. Why we are here. Is this true?"

"Yes, absolutely!" Nicky Neill leaned forward in his chair.

"We are observing a contest, a struggle, if you will, between these two aspects of human nature. As population increases and technology advances, the struggle will escalate. A jewel is only a jewel until it is not."

"Helen, I'm still not sure I understand. I feel something but I just can't...grasp it."

"What do you feel?" She reached out and laid a hand upon his shoulder.

"I, uh...I feel like you're talking about something really important, like the most important thing in the world...I think. Maybe?"

"Hmm. Good. I want you to have this." She withdrew an object from the folds of her skirt and extended it to him. "Ploox has a special necklace; I want you to have this one."

"What is it?" Nicky Neill took the item and explored it with his fingers. "Is it Mayan?"

"No, it's a fragment of a meteorite that fell to Earth. It is lifeless, and jagged, and millions of years old. It is our common future or our common past. It is not a jewel." She rose from her chair and took the necklace from Nicky Neill. She carefully placed it over his head, around his neck. "You must never forget anything, Nicholas. Ever. You are one of us now."

"Huh? Helen, I need..."

"You need," she interrupted, "to return to bed." She kissed his forehead and turned him about by the shoulders. "Go. We'll meet again."

Nicky Neill spun about to confront her, but she was gone. The smell of laundry soap filled his nostrils. Somewhere, beyond the wall, a dog barked. Nicky Neill retraced his steps to his room. When he was beneath his blanket, he reached for the odd necklace Helen had given him, but he fell asleep before his fingers could examine it a second time.

CHAPTER 81

*E*dwards Jane, the college president's own pilot, taxied the aircraft out of the fallow cornfield onto the dirt road that angled east from town and waved his passengers over. He left the pilot's seat and opened the cabin door. With a practiced motion he flipped the staircase down with the toe of his shoe and ushered his charges inside.

At least half the town of Palenque lined the runway, awaiting the takeoff of their very own celebrity guests. When the plane's propellers whirred at blinding speed and the engine revved to a deafening volume, the spectators began to cheer and wave deliriously. Ploox and Nicky Neill pressed their noses to a single window and scanned the crowd for their friends. The Campo family was nowhere in sight.

Edwards Jane fully engaged the throttle and the aircraft hurtled down the roadway at breakneck speed. As the nose of the plane began to lift away from the earth, the boys caught sight of a colorful banner held high by Margarita and Rosa. The banner read: AMINUEVOS PARA SIEMPRE. Señora Campo and Abuelita stood proudly beside Margarita. Constancia was pressed against Rosa, hiding her face from the morning sun. At the very end of the line of well-wishers and citizens, Jorge stood ramrod straight, one hand cocked over his eyebrow in a crisp salute.

The plane next touched down on a small government runway outside of Brownsville, Texas, where they refueled and cleared U.S. Customs. Memories of a shootout flooded the boys' minds. Ploox and Nicky Neill looked hard into one another's eyes. Not a word was uttered. From Brownsville they continued on to Oklahoma City to refuel a final time.

Back in the air once again, Nicky Neill studied the landscape beyond his window. He was excited to be on red Oklahoma soil again but he was depressed at the same time—there was not a single banana tree in sight, not even a spindly palm. In the space of a few hours, they had gone from tropical jungle to windswept plains.

"Hey, Nicky Neill! Lookit down there! What the heck is goin' on?" Ploox's forehead was plastered to the window. His index finger strained to poke through the double glass barrier.

"You better check this out, Nicky Neill!" Phin's voice cracked from excitement. "There's a jillion people down there!"

Nicky Neill crowded in beside his brother and ogled the curious scene below.

"Holy smoke bombs!" Ploox gasped in disbelief. "There's a ton o' people in the parkin' lot an' a whole mess of 'em spillin' onta the runway! Whut gives?"

The normally deserted airport was bursting with activity. The parking lot overflowed with cars. A fire engine, with lights flashing, stood alongside the runway near the control tower. A string of police cars lined the entryway to the passenger terminal. Most curious of all, however, was the presence of a Bluebird school bus parked opposite the fire engine.

"Oh, m'gosh!" Ploox muttered. "Oh, m'gosh!"

The plane landed smoothly and skimmed over the seamless concrete before stopping in front of the terminal.

"You're here, boys!" Mr. Jane announced. "Time to face the music!"

When the cabin door popped open, the Waterville Junior High band launched into the school song and the crowd of people surging at the metal fence burst into a common chant.

"HE-ROES! HE-ROES! HE-ROES! HE-ROES!"

Mr. Jane leaned in between Nicky Neill and Ploox.

"I believe those folks are here for you two. Go on!" he shouted over the roar. "Don't disappoint 'em!"

"He's right." Dr. Carpenter nodded. "This is your moment, fellas. Enjoy it."

Ploox moved toward the open door. Before he passed through he reached back and grabbed Nicky Neill's hand. They squeezed past the opening and hit the concrete together, arms above their heads. School buddies and total strangers immediately mobbed them. The mass of celebrants ushered the boys to a makeshift platform stationed beside the parking lot. Macklin Millen, Waterville's longest serving mayor, was waiting behind a podium in the middle of the stage, where he waved the boys on board. After a sensational introduction, Mr. Millen delivered a welcome home speech that continued to stoke the crowd for a full ten minutes. When he surrendered the podium, Dr. Carpenter and the rest of the family joined Ploox and Nicky Neill on the platform. Dr. Bennell, the college president, approached the microphone.

"Before I offer my two cents worth," he paused and scanned the crowd, "officers, would a few of you fellas mind escorting the Plucowski family up here?" At that moment, George Plucowski vowed to go to college one day. Dr. Bennell went on to say some wonderful things about family and sacrifice, and courage, and seeing the world. But he cut his words short when he observed the kids in the band fidgeting uncomfortably in their wool uniforms. Straightaway, they launched

"The long road home ends

into the fight song and all decorum evaporated into a back-slapping, feel-good red carpet event.

In the end, the Carpenters were swept into a caravan, preceded by a police escort, and accompanied right to their front door. A company of Marine Corps veterans, with much less fanfare, conveyed Ploox and his family home.

...   .

The first few weeks back in Waterville found the boys in constant demand. Invitations came in for photo opportunities, speaking engagements, and initiations into all kinds of organizations. That first week alone, the pair made appearances at the American Legion Post, the Moose Lodge, the YMCA, two retirement homes, the hospital, the Chamber of Commerce, and four different church youth groups. They took it all in stride. Learning to cope with celebrity felt like an extension of their life on the road.

More than anything, the boys longed to be out with their friends and schoolmates who demanded to hear their story from beginning to end. When they were lucky enough to make that happen, the results were always curious. Those kids who had known Ploox for most of his life found themselves taken aback by the changes in his personality. Former tormentors also held him in awe; so much, in fact, that he once confided to Nicky Neill he almost liked them better the old way. He was quick to stress the "almost" part, however.

in fanfare and adulation"

In spite of the jubilant homecoming, both boys shared a secret preoccupation. At the end of each day, they found themselves nervously addressing the fate of Hector and the Lacandon. Nicky Neill was equally concerned about the lost world within the mountain. To his complete surprise, he also found himself worrying about the fearsome Jaguar Man. He, Ploox, One-Zero, and even his dad had upset a delicate balance. He understood now that every action had a consequence. He hoped that this one would not be too severe.

...   .

On the day that marked their first full week back in Oklahoma, Dr. Carpenter came home early and summoned Nicky Neill into his office. There, they called Ploox and insisted he join them as soon as possible. When Ploox arrived, Mrs. Carpenter escorted him to the study and closed the door behind him.

"Men," Dr. Carpenter began, "I received a telegram this afternoon from the governor of Chiapas state...in Mexico. I want to share this news with you."

"Uh, should we sit down, Mr. C?" Ploox began taking short, choppy breaths.

"Sure, George. Of course, pull up a chair. You, too, son." When both boys were comfortably settled, he withdrew the telegram from his shirt pocket. "The governor says here that upon review of our experience in the jungle, he has decided to declare a moratorium on all visits and undertakings, scientific or otherwise, in that particular region."

"Whut's that mean, egzactly?" Ploox spoke up. "Yuh know, the 'morastory' thing..."

"Moratorium means he's putting a hold on all requests to visit the area." Dr. Carpenter smiled and nodded approvingly. "No one, at least not officially, will be venturing into Lacandon territory."

"It means," Nicky Neill joined in, "that Hector and the Lacandon are in the clear. No one, not outsiders, not the army, and not the police—nobody is going in there anytime soon."

"So," Ploox grinned, "ain't nobody gonna bug them folks. They'll be able ta git their lives back an' maybe even rebuild muh, uh, whoops, *their* palace!"

"And the lost world will stay lost. Right, Dad?"

"That's correct, son. We didn't bring the house down and we can all be grateful for that."

···   ···   ···

As the summer grew short, Nicky Neill took to spending more and more of his free time at the public library. He began a research effort to learn about the world's tropical forests. He was quick to discover why One-Zero and Helen were so concerned. His inquiry expanded. Soon he was investigating other issues, oceans in particular, and later, water in general. For the first time that he could remember, he looked forward to the beginning of school. There were a lot of things he wanted to know.

Ploox developed a few new habits himself. Chief among them was the practice of reading. He and Nicky Neill rode their bikes together to the library but they did not usually return home together. A certain young volunteer, a seventh grader by the name of Becky Bristow, had captured Ploox's attention. Her walk home each afternoon was a long one, and it led her across the railroad tracks east of town. This area of Waterville had a rough reputation. Consequently, Ploox took it upon himself to escort her on her hike. It was, he liked to say, the gentlemanly thing to do. He was also quick to add that walking Becky home didn't mean he wasn't still in love with Margarita. That, he insisted, was forever.

— The End —

ABOUT THE AUTHORS

The Brothers Armfinnigan are Neill and David Armstrong.

Neill has been a dreamer and a vagabond for most of his life. He has been an athlete, a soldier, a global traveler, a spinner of tales, and a perpetual lover of life. He is currently a professor engaged in teacher preparation in Deep East Texas. Neill lives outside the oldest town in Texas with his wife, Jody, and his three youngest children. Writing and telling the tales of Ploox and Nicky Neill have been a labor of love.

David "Mo" Armstrong has called the prairies of southern Alberta home for the past forty years. He taught elementary school in the town of Claresholm until his retirement in 2008. From the time he and Neill began writing *Adventures With Ploox* in 1981, he would read the latest version to his students. The Brothers eventually had the story they wanted, the story that is now yours to share.

Mo lives with his wife, Jane, at Barley Acres, where they raised their two children. Scanning the prairies from his tree house and swapping yarns with visitors remains a favorite activity.

ABOUT THE ARTIST

Having entered the world at the same time the Brothers began *Adventures With Ploox*, Beau Brown Armstrong has been a lifelong fan of these tales, and is thrilled to provide some graphic interpretation in these first editions through covers and illustrations. He currently finds himself working with digital film and media in Stockholm, Sweden, but remains a proud graduate of the arts from Oklahoma State University. Like Ploox and Nicky Neill, he is always ready for adventure.

fenny on...

CPSIA information can be obtained at www.ICGtesting.com
Printed in the USA
LVOW10s1038181115

463036LV00006B/282/P